the
DOOR
in the
MOUNTAIN

a tragedy

Special thanks to:

Kim Lund
Pete Hunt

ISBN: 1543197728
ISBN-13: 978-1543197723

For the Openshaws

CONTENTS

1. THE BIRTH OF A TAX COLLECTOR

June looked through her mother's jewelry box for some trinket to complement her rather plain dress. The box was of decent size, yet it was quite barren on the inside, a testament to something June so often forgot—her family was poor. Despite the slim pickings, she inspected each piece, knowing one of them would surely work, before finally settling upon a shiny black crystal set in stiff strands of gold.

Slipping it upon her finger, she pulled her shoulders back and flattened out the front of her dress again. It was a dull green dress, the color of grass in autumn, that puffed out at the shoulders and collar in a style June had only seen on older women.

Newer fashions had come and gone since then, leaving the rippled shoulders behind long ago. With many, if not all, of the city councilors sure to attend, June's dress would not be the most elegant at the ceremony, but it was better than most would expect for a pipe-fitter's daughter.

She extended her hand and admired the ring upon it, trying to imagine what both the ring and dress looked like on her. She had trouble imagining it, but knew she liked how the jewel looked on her hand. It was a hand that had already seen the inside of many pocketbooks and would soon be welcome to many more.

Leaving the mostly empty box of jewels, June went to the kitchen, unhooking the family's copper pot from the wall beyond the table. It stood upright in her outstretched hands as June strained to see her reflection in the tawny metal. Having never had a mirror in the house, it was a trick she and her sister, Tansy, had learned long ago.

"Don't fret, dear," her mother said. "You look like one of *them*." She sat in the corner, needle in hand, mending some unknown textile. Considering her husband's line of work, June's mother was always occupied with extending the life of the clothing the pipe-fitter seemed intent on destroying.

"Them?"

"Oh, you know—the big people. All their clothes look like that, except they have the tailors sew in extra deep pockets." Her father, resting his eyes in a chair opposite his wife, stuck his thumb into his chest. "The only difference between us and them is how muddy our shoes are. But if I had to choose between looking like this or looking like that," he pointed over

8

to June in her dress of leafy lush, "I'd say she's made the right choice." Knowing her old dress to be quite fancy to her parents, she could only nod in modest thanks.

A timid knock came through the door, and June's mother set down the needle and cloth. "At last."

June opened the door to reveal not the chief constable, whose knock they were expecting, but her Duncan. June could taste the city air flowing in with him as he crossed the threshold and she moved quickly to keep the cool of autumn from stealing what little heat the thin wattled walls of the Gladwell house had managed to keep in on such a windy day. Once inside, Duncan let loose the cloak he held bundled around him. He was a head taller than June but his slim shoulders kept him from looking his full twenty years. Try as he might to pretend otherwise, Duncan was still possessed of that boyish youth the city would inevitably grind from him, as it did most. June knew she would be there to see it happen. She would watch slowly, as all wives do, as the whimsy in his eyes grew more and more dull each day, until there was nothing left but a man.

But for now, he was her boy and she was his girl, and the whimsy was yet alive, and though Duncan's knock was not the one they waited for she was still glad to see him.

He greeted her parents in their corners as he shook his head and relaxed his shoulders, obviously grateful to be off the windy street. "Uncle Hector's going to the ceremony after all, so I'll have to stay at the library while he's gone. I just wanted to stop in and wish you luck."

"Luck? It's a graduation, Dun. It's a sure thing."

"As sure as the bookkeeper's sums?"

"As sure as the library's hums." She smiled, as she did every time they spoke their words together. The verse was meaningless to others, of course, as the young lovers had invented the rhyme for themselves—a passing reference to Duncan's uncle, Hector, who often sang to himself while he worked in the lifeless aisles of the library.

He returned her smile. "I'm just sorry I can't be there and wanted you to know I'll be thinking about you."

Even when Duncan could not be there, he still somehow managed to send his heart with her. He had always been like that, ever since they first met as small children attending their lessons. He himself credited his father for that part of himself, though June had never had a chance to meet the man. But from what Duncan told her, she could see how he had ended up as compassionate and loving as he did.

He had been a guild man of quite some acclaim in the politics of Titus Bay, sympathetic to the plights of the common citizens and an outspoken opponent to the taxes that burdened the city. But the summer cough took him, as it does so many, and he left Duncan with no mentor to follow into the guilds—a hard path for any would-be apprentice.

Meanwhile, Hector Emerick, the head curator of the city library and brother to Duncan's mother, had never married and had no children. With no one in line to take over the library after him, for such positions were reserved for distant relatives of the appointed city leaders, Hector had taken it upon himself to train the boy.

This would eventually present a problem for the

young lovers, of course. Had Duncan been raised to work in the guilds, they would have made a perfectly acceptable match, for June's own father was of the guilds himself. But the office of curator was that of the appointed, and distant though Duncan's relation was, marriage to someone from the lowest of the guilds would have been unacceptable to the city council. The council approved all marriages in Titus Bay and would certainly be sensitive to losing the head curator position to an even more distant and tenuously related family. There were so few appointed offices within the city, and in only sixty short years since Lord Titus the leadership hierarchy was already bursting at the seams for all the sprawling families that clamored to legitimize their place in high society.

Such politics of Ashmere might have doomed their fledgling love if not for Chief Constable Eastberry and Cale the Counter, the latter of whom had taken her into training at the behest of the former. Caleb Nortingale was the bookkeeper for the Union of Guilds, an office held only by one person at a time, with an assistant groomed to assume the role when the time came.

June had been selected for the training when she was fifteen and had spent five years in study and preparation for the job, and the graduation ceremony that evening would mark the end of her training. She would go in a student and come out the assistant bookkeeper for the Union of Guilds. She would no longer be a pipe-fitter's daughter. The ceremony would elevate her to that of the Union—the top tier of the guilds, and certainly an eligible match for the city librarian, when Duncan's time came to take over for his uncle.

After Duncan left, the three of them went back to waiting. It was the chief constable's knock they expected, for he had promised to accompany them to the Union banquet hall, for all the Gladwells, June included, were a nervous lot when forced out of their element. They were not accustomed to attending such events, for they were not the type of citizens to ever be celebrated. But the chief constable had singlehandedly changed that, and just as he had ushered her onto this new path so long ago, June knew he would see her through to the end. Until then she just had to wait, each second growing more anxious than the last.

When the knock finally came, June rushed to the door and was met with a wide smile and raised eyebrows—the incredulous face of the chief constable looking down at her. He was at least two hands taller than Duncan, and spindly all around.

"I wondered if you were still coming, Uncle Ly," she said.

He ignored her, instead putting his arm around her shoulder. "That is simply a fantastic dress, Juniper." He looked over to her father in the corner. "Arche, you didn't steal that for her, did you?"

"They don't let me near shops that sell such nice things. I hear Nortingale gave her coin for it."

"Oh is he giving you a wage before you've even graduated?"

June shook her head. "No, he just felt bad he couldn't be there tonight. He's gone out to the western mining camps on business and won't be back for quite some time."

"And what business does he have out in the mining camps? The miners aren't a guild of the

Union."

June shrugged her shoulders. "You must think I ask more questions than I do. Shall we go now?"

The chief constable crossed the room and sat next to her mother. He leaned toward her, "Does she look nervous to you? It's hard to watch, really. June, perhaps we ought to wait until you're calm and collected. We don't have to be there right away. There's plenty of time. It is, after all, a ceremony for every Union graduate, not just the new bookkeeper. It always takes quite some time to read through all those names."

June opened the door again. "Well I'd like to be there when they read mine, if you don't mind."

The three rose from their seats and went through the door she held open. The chief constable poked her side as he passed. "I'm telling you, June, nobody will miss you if you just want to skip the whole thing. Nobody's ever excited at the birth of another tax collector, especially in times like these."

He was poking fun, but June knew what he said was not far from the truth. The Union of Guilds had been created to bridge the gap between the guilds and the appointed city leaders. The bookkeepers were there to watch over the books of the guilds and ensure that all were paying proper taxes.

The Gladwells lived in the western reaches of Titus Bay, just past where the city's cobbled streets turned to dirt. Beyond, the highway wound its way west to the steep mountains that kept the country hidden and cut off from the old world. With no true destination at its end, for the mining camps of the west had long since moved north to the lower foothills, it was the least traveled of the five highways that found their intersection at Titus Bay's central square.

As they stepped out, they found the sky covered in grey clouds that smelled of impending rain, and the wind moaned as it rushed through the alleys and whistled through the loose bricks of the corners. Citizens were closing their shops and retiring for the night. Unlike June and her party, who were making their way toward the center of the city, most were making their way outward. As they passed, a crew of builders were throwing their tools down for the day, almost as if in disgust. For a moment, as they turned to follow along the cobble not far behind them, June thought she saw an even greater look of relief upon their faces, a restless gratitude for night and time of their own.

"I don't know that I've ever seen someone want to go home so badly as those men."

"It's not just them," her Uncle Ly said. "Rumor is that many of the builders are having a hard time with this new wood of the tree-cutters. It's too soft, doesn't join like normal wood. And its grain is too loose for nails to get a good bite. They'll have to get used to it, though."

"Why's that? Can't they just use the other trees?"

"As the tree-cutters clear the forests they're planting only this new spring oak of theirs. It grows faster and straighter, meaning they can harvest more of it each year. They're still harvesting the old wood, for now, and charging a premium for it, but in a few years, there won't be any left."

June did not respond, though she knew the truth of what he said. All over Titus Bay the frustrations of the tree-cutters' new oak was undeniably evident. The smiths and glass-makers complained the wood did not burn hot enough, while crews of the builders had been forced to expand in order to properly manage the dangerously pliable wood. Even at a passing glance over the city, June could tell which buildings had been made of the curious oak. Their walls bowed outward, as if struggling to hold up the sky.

June was brought back to the moment by shouts from a crowd ahead of them on the road. There were dozens of them out in front of some shop, gathered too tightly to see through to the object of their fascination. The chief constable gave the gathering a wide berth as he led June and her parents to the opposite side of the road, not breaking his gaze ahead for even a moment.

Her father noticed too. "Looks like a rowdy group, Ly. What's that all about?"

"Last night the city council approved the new tax on candles, and today every candle-maker in Titus Bay raised their prices."

"It sounded like more than a disagreement over the price of a candle to me."

The chief constable sighed. "Yes, well, I'm hoping the outrage will blow over quickly. I told the council to give them a few days before we start dispersing angry crowds." As per the appointment of Lord Titus some sixty years before, Chief Constable Eastberry was the sole law man in Ashmere, an office he inherited from his father. Though he technically worked under the direction of the city council and the magistrates, matters of crime and keeping the peace were usually left to him and his deputies, citizens whom he charged in times of need.

There were rarely any times of true need, of

course, as Ashmere had known such little crime in the decades since Lord Titus. When he did charge a deputy, however, it was usually because a matter called him beyond the city. As safe and free from crime as the city was, the appointment of Lord Titus dictated that the law must always remain in Titus Bay, and thus through his deputies the chief constable stayed true to his office.

The sun was nearly down, and June tried to keep her mind from wandering as they approached the banquet hall. She did not want to dwell on the problems of the builders, nor of the candle-makers. Tonight was to be her night.

2. THE CROSSED QUILLS

As formal as the occasion was, June found the Union banquet hall to be more comfortable than expected. Long woven banners hung from the vaulted walls, each bearing the mark of a trade guild, and the maroon color of the adornments, only now beginning to fade with age, made the space feel warmer and much more intimate.

Rows and rows of benches filled one end of the long and narrow hall, and June and company filed in where they found space toward the front. Facing the audience were seated the leaders of the Union, those guildmasters of the most influential guilds in Ashmere. This was one of few such events that warranted the presence of no appointed, as guild and union business was no business of theirs. The guilds had formed as a response to the power Lord Titus had entrusted to the appointed—power that was, in their view, often used to overreach. The candle tax was only the latest in a series that seemed designed to drain the guilds of any profits, and though June had only recently become old enough to care, she knew well the tension that was growing between the guilds and the city council.

When the shuffling of attendants finding their seats finally ceased, the speaker of the ceremony, Julian Yeates, stood. June had met him before, but knew little of the legend save what she had heard from others. They called him the First Merchant of Ashmere, and his great age seemed to fit the title. As she examined the creases in his face and the ancient furrow of his brow, she knew she had only ever seen one person who could perhaps rival his years—her neighbor Mira, the recluse.

But unlike June's neighbor who rarely left her home, Julian still carried himself like a younger man with something to prove. He was not only still the head of the merchants' guild, but also served as the head of the Union itself. And though he was not appointed, he had been at the forefront of the protests that lead to the allowance of guild formations within the hidden country. This was all decades before June was born, of course, but she recognized that many things she thought normal were brought about by this ancient man.

He stood at the dark walnut podium for a moment, silent as dawn breaking on the mountains. Though his figure was gaunt and peaked, June could see the true man contained in the shell through his eyes. He still had his full bearing, perhaps even more than most others did in their prime.

He took off his thin copper spectacles and held them up for all to see. "Believe it or not, there was once a time when Titus Bay had no glass-makers. In fact, throughout all of Ashmere there were no thatchers, builders, smiths, masons, pipe-fitters, or tanners. From far across the south sea King Vener had summoned Ashmere to fight in his great war, and for years not a man between sixteen and sixty remained.

"And when Lord Titus came and declared the war over and Ashmere free of any fealty to Vener, he saved our hidden country not only by returning its sons and husbands, but by recovering its industry. Had they not returned, their crafts might have been lost forever. That all of you are in this room is not only a testament to Lord Titus, but to those craftsmen, your grandfathers, who passed their skills down to you.

"From birth every citizen of Ashmere, in varying capacity, is called to contribute to what Lord Titus established on that fateful day of his return. We in this room are the commerce of the hidden country. We in this room are the builders and the creators. If the appointed were called to lead as the hand of Lord Titus, then surely we are legs by which Ashmere stands and moves forward."

The elder gestured toward the banquet tables beyond the rows of benches whereon sat his audience. "We are here this evening to celebrate all of you. You have all worked hard to master your crafts, and though many of you are of different guilds, you are all now of the Union. With that, we'll now begin the advancement."

For most of the others in the room, the advancement was but a formality. Within their respective guilds, most of them had already advanced from apprentice to journeyman. Such functions for them were put on by the Union in hopes of keeping the disparate guilds familiar one with another and fostering a degree of comradery between them. Unlike them, June was not advancing to journeyman status. She was not even of the guilds; as bookkeeper she was *only* of the Union.

A new speaker stood at the podium and called on each guild to present their advancing journeyman, and one by one the young craftsmen came forward. There were but two other girls among them, for the trade guilds were mainly composed of men. Depending on the nature of the craft, most women who came into guild work only found entrance by learning from their husbands. June had even known some to be formally accepted into a guild only after being widowed and proving themselves to have sufficient knowledge of the craft to continue making a living.

When all the guilds had presented their newest members, the speaker called on the Union itself. Only one other stood with June, a younger boy, presumably as good at sums as she or better, to join the ranks of the city surveyors. Together the two of them approached the speaker at the podium and stood still before the audience while the unsteady hands of the First Merchant of Ashmere attached the pins that denoted a Union worker.

June touched the pin that now hung at her breast. It was gold formed into the shape of two crossed quills, the meticulous workmanship unlike anything June had ever seen. Only two people at a time ever wore such a pin—and now she was one of them.

The guests were then all invited to gather at the many tables in the back of the hall for the banquet, and the crowd rose and slowly made their way toward the smell of the feast. In the moving crowd June moved like a wren bouncing among the leaves and caught up to her parents, who each hugged her.

She then threw her arms around the chief constable. "Thank you for everything, Uncle Ly. This is all because of you."

"I didn't do anything, my dear. You did all the work and you earned this for yourself."

This was, of course, not entirely true. It had been the chief constable who had, all those years before, noticed June's affinity for sums and had recommended her to Cale the Counter. He had taken some convincing, June remembered, for there were many others vying for the newly-opened spot, many who were more prime for the position than she. Recommendations had poured into Cale's Union office from every direction, and distant cousins and friends of friends were showing up at his doorstep to introduce their children. Several times had the chief constable even taken June to visit the Counter. She had never asked what finally convinced the man to choose her, but she assumed the chief constable had pulled some strings he had been saving for quite some time.

They were strings he gladly pulled, she knew. For as long as June could remember, her father having made good friends with the chief constable well before her birth, the Gladwells and the Eastberrys were all but family. She even called him *uncle* and thought of his children as her cousins. In this sense, it was not so surprising that he would stick his neck out to help her into the Union.

Above the other appointed leaders, the chief constable was perhaps the most sympathetic to the plight of the common citizen. He was well aware of the struggles of his friend, the pipe-fitter, and though sympathetic as he may have been, his appointed office came with none of the power or influence bestowed upon the mayor and city councilors. The only way to help his friend enjoy a better life was to help better the lot of his children.

It was this for which June thanked the tall man with the golden cord of the chief constable draped across his chest. The path may have been hers, but June could never have found her way to it alone.

The air of the banquet was light and merry, with the wafting smells of the feast carrying away any thoughts of the city beyond the walls of the Union hall. The centers of the tables were covered in platters of venison and heavily salted beef roasts, surrounded by all manner of sweet pastries and pies. When June had enjoyed her fill, she left her parents and the chief constable and joined Duncan's uncle Hector who was seated nearby.

Hector's table seated what few of the city administration had bothered to attend the event, most of them only nodding acquaintances to June. They all smiled and congratulated her as she sat next to Hector.

Edmond Dayse, of the city surveyors, looked briefly from her to the surrounding tables. "Where's the bookkeeper proper? It seems like he should certainly be here."

"He left three days ago for a visit to the mining

camps in the western foothills."

"What does that mean for your work? How are you to begin without the Counter here?"

"Oh, I've already been working under him for some time, but now his supervision will be a bit looser than before. He's actually given me quite a list of things to do while he's gone, so I won't have a problem staying busy."

"Well, I'm glad to hear he's traveling. I was afraid he might have taken ill. From what I understand the summer cough this year is an especially bad one."

From beside her, Hector spoke. "They say the Mayor Norfolk's been down in his bed with the cough for months now. The fevers are returning to him almost daily and with each one he's struck more and more delirious. He doesn't know where he is and doesn't respond to his poor wife when she speaks to him."

"I wonder if he has any clue how the city council is wreaking havoc on the citizens in his absence."

"Would it matter if he did? The appointed councilors passed the candle tax unanimously, with the three guildmasters casting the only dissenting votes. There may be some strength in the mayor's office, but he doesn't have much power over the collective council. And let's be honest—he would have probably been in favor of the tax anyway."

"Did you see the display at the Burning Wick today? The candle-makers have just taken the cost of the new tax and added it to the price of their candles. Everyone's whipped into a frenzy over it."

"They are, of course, directing the citizens' wrath to those leaders who approved the tax. If the city council isn't careful they're going to have real trouble on their hands. His vote may align with the council more often than not, but the man has charisma and he's loved by the citizens. With the mayor so terribly ill the council has no one to calm down the angry masses."

"You know, Tinkin did mention to me whispers of secret gatherings, talk of rebellion."

"I find that hard to believe. Over a few trivial taxes?"

"Who knows? They're just whispers after all. Tinkin hears many things throughout the city. But at any rate, the chief constable and his deputies do seem to be out in full force lately, have they not? Likely on dispatch from the city council to root out the would-be rebels."

June spoke. "I don't know about any talk of rebellion, but the Circle of Scholars is stirring the minds of the citizens. I've heard that groups of citizens are simply gathering to discuss their research, and I don't blame them. Have you seen any of their research? Simply incredible."

Though the Circle of Scholars was still news to many, June had been fascinated by their emergence for months. According to their anonymous publications, the Circle was a collection of inquisitive citizens who, through exhaustive research, had uncovered convincing evidence concerning the door in the mountain.

When Lord Titus had handed his mantle to his appointed leaders, it was said that he left Ashmere through a door that led under the mountains to the old world. As long as the bay, the shape of which hid Ashmere from view of the southern sea, remained closed and all seafaring vessels illegal, the Last Lord of Ashmere had promised to return when the old world was once again safe.

Not taking his promise lightly, the citizens had accepted their secluded safety with gratitude, not venturing beyond the hidden bay or searching for the door. In fact, until the Circle of Scholars began nailing their printed research to the messengers' posts throughout the city, June had never even heard the story. She had asked her parents, but even they, having been born a decade after Lord Titus, remembered very little of the tale.

"I'd love to get my hands on one of the publications," said Dayse.

"I would too," June said, "but it's nearly impossible to know which morning will bring new pages. I try to keep an eye out as I pass through the square each morning, but I'm never early enough to see it before they tear it down. The appointed are so quick to destroy what they can that I just have to settle for what I hear second hand."

Hector put his fork down and looked at her. "Why, June, I had no idea you were interested in such things."

"I enjoy the intrigue of it, I suppose. It's as if Ashmere is learning things it long ago forgot about itself."

The feast continued well into the late evening, and June moved from table to table, visiting with what few colleagues she knew at the Union and acquaintances she had made from the guilds—folk with whom she would soon become quite intimate and who would grow to loathe her presence as they already did Cale the Counter. When the food grew cold and the smells of festivity waned, the clerks carried whatever uneaten food remained to the kitchen behind the hall, and the guests filed out into the square. Those who lived across the river walked toward the bridge at the south end of the square and others who lived closer stood around in the night air to finish their conversations before bidding one another farewell.

As June moved through the crowd to meet with her parents and Lyman, who would be saying goodnight to cross the river himself, she felt a hand on her shoulder. It was Hector, gesturing for her to step off to the side with him.

Away from the others loitering in the dark, he spoke in a hushed tone so that no one could overhear. "I thought you might be interested to know that over the past months a small group of citizens *has* managed to gather all the publications of the Circle of Scholars. I'm a member of this group, you see, but it's very hush-hush. We meet quite often and discuss many things, most relating to their research and our ideas for improving our city. If you want to read the findings for yourself, you ought to come."

"I'd be delighted. How have I not heard of these meetings from you already?"

His eyes looked to where the chief constable stood with her parents. "Because the appointed are so fervent in their efforts to silence the Circle, we think it wise to act and move with the utmost discretion. It's safest to keep our gathering small, but if you're up for it, come to the east wing just before sunset tomorrow." He left her then with a brisk step across the square toward his home behind the library.

Seeing June come to her parents, the chief constable congratulated her again and disappeared into the meandering crowd. The three then made their own way to the west highway and followed it toward their home, and as her father complained about eating roe deer and mused over a time when real stags could still be found in Ashmere, June found her thoughts wandering.

Could she be wrong about the Circle of Scholars? She did not yet know what their publications actually contained, but Hector had made it clear that their mere discussion of its contents was not to reach Lyman's ear. She had not before considered the fact that the one destroying the anonymous publication was likely her very own Uncle Ly.

The length of highway leading to their home was too short that night, and June struggled to sort her thoughts on the matter. She wondered if her interest in such forbidden gatherings was a betrayal to her uncle, a man to whom she owed so much already. And as her head lay softly upon the feathers of her pillow she saw the great stags of the old forest gather around Lord Titus, that giant man in uniform as red as dawn, and for just the briefest of moments before she slipped away into sleep, June considered not going.

3. A WALK TO
TITUS'S GRAVE

The night was receding at the first hints of impending dawn when a slight but steady rapping at June's window woke her. Lifting the shutters, she found Duncan. To be woken in such a fashion was nothing new, for Duncan had taken to knocking on her shutters instead of the door. He did not do this out of secrecy, but out of consideration for her sleeping parents in the next room. They were old enough that no one would bat an eye at any concerns of impropriety. In a country as small as Ashmere, one with messengers like Tinkin gathering every rumor and interest of the citizens, all secrets eventually come to light.

"Let's go for a walk," he whispered. "We can go watch the sunrise."

She met him outside and together they started down the cobblestone leading east into the center of the city. Titus Bay was a city that retired early and rose late. Whether it was a smith or a glass-maker readying their furnace for the day June could not be sure, but the smell of morning embers was the only sign of life to be had.

Their steps were slow as the lovers made their way to their favorite spot. Duncan asked her about the graduation, sorry to have missed her moment of triumph but eager to recover the loss. She reassured him that all he missed was good food.

As she reviewed the events of the night her step stuttered and she paused, debating whether or not to ask her next question. "Do you know of any gatherings after dark in the east wing of the library? Hector mentioned they've had a few in the past, but acted like they were to be kept secret."

"If there were gatherings after the library closes, I wouldn't know about it. We clean after we lock up, and I do only the west wing. He does the east."

She told him more of the previous night's discussion of the Circle of Scholars and his uncle's interest in the subject. As Duncan thought it over he told her the only person he had ever noticed come to the library after hours was Cale the Counter. This, of course, had not ever raised any questions in Duncan, for Hector and Cale were known to be close friends. And ever since his wife's passing some years before, Cale was wont to stop by the library often to visit.

Both June and Duncan were talkers, and their conjecture over the strange happenings in the east wing provided plenty of material for morning conversation. By the time they reached the stairs leading down to their spot near the docks the sun was nearly over the eastern mountains.

Still standing but certainly on their last legs, the docks were relics of a time lost but not yet quite forgotten—a time when Ashmere still looked outward to know its place in the world. The old lighthouse, standing high upon the cliffs east of Titus Bay, had not shone its great light for sixty years. Without its beacon reaching out over the narrow waters that bent to link the bay to the south sea, the country was hidden from the world. Any ship deliberately searching for Ashmere would almost certainly never find the bay's entrance, and a ship with no such intention would never happen upon it by chance.

It was all done in the wisdom of Lord Titus, of course. He had returned from the great war no more a man loyal to his king, but a man loyal to his people. He burnt the lighthouse and the ships in the bay to make sure the great war would never reach their land. Still bearing black scars from the charring, the docks were the last visible sign of his handiwork within the city, though the ruins of the lighthouse still stood without.

They slowly tread down to where the grey and warped wood of the docks met the stone walkway. At the bottom of the steps stood the monument many called *Titus's Grave*. It was not a proper grave, of course, for everyone knew that Lord Titus had not died the way most men do. Instead, when he felt his work was finished, he appointed the families that would rule in his absence and disappeared into the foothills, promising to return to open the bay when the old world was safe again. The grave had been erected soon after, a thick block of stone that looked outward over the water so that anyone reading it was facing the city.

The morning light was soon coming, but it was still fairly dark, and in the shadow of the eastern mountains they stood before the epitaph, just able to make out the words inscribed into its surface, though they knew them well from countless morning strolls:

Look forth and behold undying monument
To Titus
The First and Last Lord of Ashmere
Who proved faithful to all trust of his country and his
people
And who saved them from the tyranny of the old world.
To all generations who seek his testament,
Strike forth and find the key to his return.

Below the words was the figure of a key, so perfectly engraved that one might have been tempted to snatch it from the stone. June always liked to run her hands over the surface, wondering how a rock could be carved so smooth.

The first light of morning broke over the city, peeking down through the streets to where June and Duncan looked at the old grave. The light was warm on her face, and she looked down to see that Duncan had taken her hand in his..

"I want to ask you something," he began. "Do you ever think about us, June?" His voice wavered as he spoke, betraying the racing of his heart. June thought she could even feel it through their clasped fingers.

"What do you mean? I think about us all the time."

He turned to face the bay and she with him. "For so long there's been something hanging over the both of us, threatening to someday keep us apart. But there isn't much left to separate us anymore. Where so many things could have gone awry, everything has lined up for us. And sooner than expected."

She tugged on his arm. "What are you saying?"

"Yesterday Uncle Hector told me he's feeling too old for his job at the library. He intends to step down quite soon—perhaps in just a matter of weeks." June threw her arms around his neck. She was not sure, but this would likely make Duncan one of the youngest city administrators in the history of Titus Bay.

She let herself down from his shoulders. "You'll make a fine head curator, Dun. You're looking more and more appointed by the minute."

Duncan, blushing, looked up to meet her gaze. "And once I'm head curator, we can be married."

She did not have time to sort her feelings in the moment. All she knew is that her heart burned warm within her chest and she could not help the smile that slowly swayed her entire expression. To say she had not thought about this over many a dizzy daydream would have been a lie—and not a good one.

"Do you really think I'd make a good librarian's wife?"

She looked up into the whimsy of the boy's eye, and he gave her a quick wink. "Oh, I don't think you'll ever be *the librarian's wife*. I think you'll always be *the bookkeeper*."

"You're right. I'm sure you'd make an acceptable

bookkeeper's husband, though."

"As sure as the library's hums?"

"As sure as the bookkeeper's sums. Come, let's head back."

June grabbed his hand and together they made their way back up the steps the way they had come. The crows of roosters near and far throughout the city followed them, and in the light of a new day the city woke up around them.

"You may look like a good curator, but let's hope you don't age like Hector. Isn't he only in his forties?"

4. A PROPOSAL IN
THE DARK

They said goodbye and kissed at June's doorstep, and Duncan walked back into the city to open the library for the day. Inside the house she found her mother and father wide awake and moving about the kitchen cleaning up. June winced at the screeching sound of her mother scraping her pan out, realizing she and Duncan had been gone longer than she realized.

"I left you a plate on the table, dear."

Egg on toast with beans was a typical breakfast in Ashmere, and no one combined them better than Garland Gladwell. A clever and capable woman in every regard, she had made sure to impart this quality into her two daughters. June liked to think her mother successful in this endeavor, though her younger sister Tansy might have caused some doubt. Luckily, Tansy had married young and moved away to the cattlelands to live with her new husband, Burl. He brought out her gifts like her own mother never could, and she took care of him well, finding herself to be quite suited to life in the north.

Such pairings between the rural and city folk were uncommon, but no one could deny that chance had worked in their favor. Wandering cows were to thank, as Tansy told it. Burl had been taking the cattle down the north highway to sell in the city, when one morning he woke to find half of them missing. He spent nearly an entire day of his journey searching the hills before he rounded them up and was able to continue. Though the rural folk have little regard for the festivities of the city, the day Burl finally reached Titus Bay was the day of the Lighthouse Festival and, finding no reason not to tarry for the night, decided to join the citizens in celebrating the famous burning of the lighthouse.

It was there at the foot of the crude recreation of the tower, where lovers in pairs came to contribute their flame, that Tansy and Burl met. They came alone to the conflagration to toss in their own burning offering, but walked away together. Even on that night, Tansy once said, there was no other fire in their eyes but what burned for one another.

As happy as the tale of Tansy was, however, it did present some frustration for Garland, whose main concern was that her younger daughter had married before her older sister. This frustration often manifested itself to June in the form of eager curiosity and even outright nosiness. That said, June certainly understood it, for her mother had passed this very trait on to her, and she too sometimes found herself completely possessed by her curiosity.

Thus June debated telling her mother about the morning's revelations, for she could only guess just how many questions she might have to endure from the woman.

The contemplation was broken by her mother. "How was your walk with Duncan?"

"He's quite overjoyed. Apparently, Hector's told him he intends to step down very soon."

"And Duncan's to take over?" She tilted her head, giving June that sideways look she expected. "When shall we plan the wedding?"

June shook her head. "We've talked about it, but it may be better to wait until he's the curator proper." She did not quite understand why, but romance was still not a comfortable topic of conversation with her parents.

"I must say I don't know what you have waited this long for" her mother said. "No one will remember in the years to come that a pipe-fitter's daughter married the librarian. And now that you're in the Union I see no reason to wait."

Her father emerged from whatever had been occupying him in the back. "To wait for what? Marriage? You better be careful, Juniper. If you're not careful you're going to end up like Old Mira." It was not the first time the name of the ancient woman had been invoked. Having lived in the next cottage over from the Gladwells, separated only by a thick grove of trees, Mira had always seemed to June something of a permanent fixture. In her old age she tended to stay inside and keep to herself, and June knew surprisingly little about her beyond the exploits of her youth, stories that everyone knew.

"I don't see why that's a bad thing. Mira's one of the most well-known and regarded names in the guilds. She established the entire glass-making trade after the great war and moved her craft forward like no other. If anything, her example should teach us that love is not the only thing that can fulfil us. We have other purposes."

"But she's nearly ninety and hasn't crafted so much as a window in twenty years. So, I ask you, what does she have now?"

June had to admit to herself that she did not know. Besides passing pleasantries on those rare occasions where she was outside, June had spoken very little to the woman and certainly dared not speak on her behalf. It was but mere hopeful conjecture to suppose that Mira still felt her life a fulfilling one. It was hard to imagine anyone could enjoy such a life, for Mira moved little in her aged frailty. But it was not always so, June thought, as she was once known to be a woman of nature who spent much of her free time beyond the reaches of the city exploring the forest. Perhaps there is a certain time for fulfillment, and those forgotten days were Mira's.

June left her home frazzled by the discussion but none the worse for wear. It was, after all, her first day wearing the crossed quills of the Union bookkeepers. Though Cale was gone beyond the city, he had left her a lengthy list of visits to make, and by the look of it she knew she had her work cut out for her. The first item on the list was labeled *The Burning Wick*, the same candle shop where June had witnessed the upheaval in the street just the day before.

That Cale was beyond the city and unable to perform this visit was almost too convenient, for given the tension surrounding the new tax, this was the one place June would rather avoid. She wondered how her superior, now on his fourth day gone, could have known about the candle tax before its announcement at the city council only two nights before. As the prime tax collector for Titus Bay, Cale was likely more privy to the workings of the council than she, and certainly under no obligation to share his secrets with her.

Unlike the evening before, June found the candle shop that morning devoid of not only a boisterous crowd, but of patrons altogether. Upon the shelves, candles of all sizes and colors stared out through the dark windows. The shop was still, and June was hesitant to enter, unsure of whether or not it was even open. Nevertheless, despite the uncertainty, June was not one to leave a task undone—especially a task written down. A resolution made to oneself is easily enough brushed aside and forgotten, but a written one is another matter entirely, and June knew too much about accounting to think this task would be overlooked by Cale when he returned.

A bell above the door announced June's entrance, though it was entirely unnecessary. The shop was entirely empty, save for a single book and a bald shopkeeper hiding behind it. He was seated just behind the counter, his eyes only leaving the book in his hands to meet hers.

He set his book down and sat up a little straighter on his stool. "It looks like a lovely day outside, Miss. I shudder to think what could tear you from it in favor of my shop."

"I've come from the Union of Guilds, sir, and I'm here to discuss the new tax with you."

"You're from the Union? Where's the Counter?" It was a question June was quite used to. Upon realizing that such a young girl had come to inspect their business and dictate their taxes, many tradesmen inquired after Cale the Counter, who could accord them some level of comfort as only a middle-aged man could. His numbers were always the same as hers, however, for even when he did choose to indulge such people, which was only on rare occasion, he would simply provide them with June's figures again.

"He's away on business, I'm afraid." She lightly touched her collar where the crossed quills were pinned. "I'm Juniper Gladwell, his assistant."

She extended her hand, and after an excruciating moment he took it. "Pleased to meet you. I'm Brand Estwick. Now, Juniper, you seem like a nice girl and I don't want to be rude, but there's really no point in going over these new taxes. I've already raised the price of my candles to make up for the added expense. I don't expect to sell a single candle, so I don't expect I'll have to pay any tax on them. Look around you—there are no customers." A fact that had not been lost on June, even before she came in.

"You seem to take pleasure in that fact."

"Oh very much so, yes. There are only six candle-makers in Titus Bay and I can assure you all of them will be joining me in this, which you're sure to find out soon enough. I expect the Counter's got you going to all them today."

"But aren't you afraid that someone else will begin

making candles and take all your business?"

He shrugged. "Do you really think anyone would venture into a craft that's more heavily taxed than others? Soon enough the whole city will be dark and when the city council is done bumbling about in the darkness they will repeal this absurd tax and we will once again light up Titus Bay. Until then—there's simply no tax to pay. If the appointed are keen on collecting more money to fund their lives, tell them to go visit their chums at the bank and deal with them the same way they deal with the rest of us."

June left the candle-maker and walked to the next tasks on her list, which were, just as the Burning Wick had supposed, his fellow candle-makers. The bulk of her day was spent in transit, making her way through the busy streets from one practitioner to the other. The visits, unlike the time it took to travel from one to the next, were quite short. Each candle-maker was nice enough, as the first had been, but they all told her the same thing: the candle-makers would not take the tax lying down.

The candle-makers' unity came as a surprise to June. In all her time working under Cale she had never interacted with them in any capacity. With only a handful of members, theirs was the smallest guild in Ashmere. But despite their small size, they were fiercely loyal to both their guild and their principles. They had evidently coordinated all of this, and though June admired their conviction, she questioned the strategy. To her it seemed obvious that by making their wares unaffordable the candle-makers were simply hurting themselves.

The sun was sinking below the western mountains when she left the last candle-maker. There was still one more to be visited, but June knew it would have to wait until tomorrow if she hoped to meet Hector at the library. With the librarian expecting her before sunset, her pace through the city was as brisk as the air of the autumn evening that was moving in off the great bay.

It was well after sunset but not entirely night when she finally came into the central square. She found the doors of the east wing were locked and the windows dark. She assumed Hector must have wanted to meet her there and lead her to where the gatherings were held; he had evidently left without her. Never one to leave a stone unturned, June reached toward the door, but before she could knock she heard the tumblers of the lock roll and the door cracked open. Behind it June could just see Hector's eyes poking around. When he saw it was her he swung the door wide.

After ushering her inside, Hector locked the door. "I had almost given up on you coming. They're a punctual lot, these ones. They've already started."

"Well, I hope nothing was delayed while you were here waiting for me."

"Oh they never wait. Luckily, I don't lead the discussions, I simply host them. Follow me."

The east wing of the library was a separate structure from the rest which stood directly across the street. It was a strange building by all counts, and June had always speculated that it had been built for some other purpose than holding books. Unlike the west wing, a grand stone building with vaulting walls, the east wing had been constructed with a mixture of stone, wood, and daubed wattle—as if it had been built in stages. It was not an extremely tall building by the standards of Titus Bay, and unlike its counterpart, the east wing was split into two floors, resulting in both having uncomfortably squat ceilings so low June could almost feel their weight on her shoulders.

Hector led her through a maze of shelves toward the steps leading upstairs. She had been in the east wing many times over the years, but when they came to the stairs she had to pause a moment to grasp what she was seeing. There below the stairs leading upward a section of shelving had been swung outward to reveal steps leading down. As she followed down the winding steps to the cellar below she could hear low grunts and murmurs of men talking, and the air was musty and thick.

The room at the bottom of the stairs was dark, and only a single lantern burned in the corner, giving what precious little light it could to the lone man standing. Before him, on various benches, chairs, and piles of books, a crowd was seated. They had obviously been engaged in lengthy discourse, though they all now turned to see who had descended upon them.

"Hector," the standing man growled. It was a familiar voice, but June, unable to discern the man's identity for the shadow, still could not place it. "What's the meaning of this? You'd bring the Union bookkeeper to spy us out?"

"She's here to discuss the Circle—just like the rest of us in here."

Another rose from his seat. "She's practically family to the chief constable."

Just when enough became enough and June decided to speak for herself, a hand caught hold of hers in the darkness. "She's practically family to us here." It was Duncan's voice defending her, speaking with a confidence that seemed nearly out of place in a secret dungeon below the library.

While Hector stepped forward and assured his fellows of their safety under his roof, June leaned over to Duncan, whom she had not expected to see. "How long have you known about this," she whispered, "and kept it from me?"

"I think when Uncle Hector invited you he assumed there was no point in hiding it from me any longer. I just found out today."

"And how's it been so far? What's happened?

"This one standing has been reading from the latest research of the Circle. They say the door was not made by Lord Titus, but existed long before. They've found some old text that says only some of the first founders of Ashmere came by ship; many others came through the door."

By then Hector had smoothed over the concerns of room, and the lot of them resumed their discourse. June listened intently to the man in the middle. He read slowly and unmistakably, occasionally lifting his eyes from the paper to look out over his audience. Here and there a citizen would ask a question, and the reader would stop to let them discuss.

Hector walked back to where June and Duncan stood near the stairs and whispered, "Don't mind Brand's temper. They don't call him the Burning Wick for nothing." June's eyes shot up to the reader, nearly voicing her surprise for all to hear. The man standing at their center was the very same candle-maker she had visited first in the morning. Her eyes focused in the darkness, and she searched the faces of the room, wondering if the other candle-makers were present, but in the weak light of the lantern could recognize none.

Off to the side, sitting just in front of the lone lantern, a man seated in the audience drew June's attention. It was not his appearance that caught her eye, for he was a stranger of somewhat nondescript appearance. It was his composure that struck her, for he seemed just as out of place as she—but of the two of them it was only June who was uncomfortable. He sat with a small group of fellows who, though they all faced the reader standing before them, almost seemed to circle around the man.

June tugged at Hector's sleeve, and he leaned over to hear her. "Who's the man in the corner?"

Hector shrugged. "I don't recognize him. Like you, he must be new to our little group."

As per what seemed to be the normal routine of the gatherings, when the candle-maker had finished with the latest publication of the Circle, he set the paper down and spoke off the cuff. "My fellows, for me and the other candle-makers this week has been, as you have all probably heard, taxing." He smiled and a few of the listeners chuckled. "I want to thank Hector for allowing this sort of gathering under his roof. In times as trying as these, it's a relief to know that not all city officers seek to preserve their power at our expense."

Amid the grunts of agreement and nodding heads following the candle-maker's words, June watched the stranger in the corner. He tapped on the arm of the man in front of him, who briefly looked back at him, before cutting into the chatter loudly.

"It's despicable what's happened to you, friend. Sickening. The council has truly overstepped their bounds with these taxes, and it's only going to get worse from here. And I don't mean just the candle tax, fellows. I mean the taxes on the miners' coal, the brick-makers' bricks, even the letters in Tinkin's satchel. The appointed have their hands in too many pockets to name, and once they've gone through every guild and tradesman at his craft they'll move on to tax us again in our homes. Let me ask you this— Do you think this is what Lord Titus had in mind for us all those years ago? Do you think he meant for the officers he appointed to abuse his people and tax them into oblivion?"

He stood before his captive audience, occasionally looking back to the silent man. "My friends, I know we're new to your gatherings, but I must say all this talk of the Circle of Scholars and the things they are finding about Lord Titus and our connection to the old world have got me yearning for the days of old when Ashmere's leaders cared about the citizens— and the citizens loved them for it. I think this candle-maker and his fellows have the right idea on how to change the will of the council, and I would propose that all of us tradesmen in this room follow suit. In protest of the excess taxes, we must cease all operations until we see something change."

Someone cut in. "And if the appointed don't cave to our demands, then what? We've all got families to feed."

"Trust me, friend. As soon as the first water-carrier refuses to fetch water for one of them, they'll be eager to discuss change."

Hector stepped forward. "Sir, I'm afraid I haven't made your acquaintance yet."

"I'm a simple spokesman, and our group here has been searching for others to gather with—a group of not just words, but action."

"Well, Spokesman, this entire discussion is not in line with the academic spirit of our gathering here. What you're proposing might be construed as treason, and I'd rather have none of it under my roof, if you don't mind."

"Not at all, good librarian. But I must point out that I'm not stirring up rebellion and I'm not advocating violence of any kind. This is merely protest I suggest, and protest is allowed under the law of Lord Titus."

"Regardless it is likely an uncomfortable prospect for many here who came tonight expecting nothing more than reading from the Circle of Scholars. But I can tell from the room there are quite a few here more oriented for action than words, and though your proposed protest is a powerful gesture, it may only be possible over the course of weeks. And if the process is going to take weeks, we might as well not put our livelihoods on the line just yet.

"You see, I myself have had an idea that's been tugging on my mind for months now—ever since I read the first publication from the Circle of Scholars—and one that should appeal to those of us who long for the days of Lord Titus."

The composure of the Spokesman grew tense, yet June could see that he tried hard to remain cordial despite his impatience. "What do you propose, good librarian?"

"We find Lord Titus."

5. TREASONOUS
TERRITORY

"Now hear me out, gentlemen." Hector raised his hands to calm the room before realizing it was still as night. The group that had been growing more and more boisterous only moments before now stared at him in silence. Perhaps they, like June, were trying to grasp the meaning behind the librarian's strange proposition.

"Before Lord Titus left he declared that he would return one day when the old world was finally safe again. But he also said he wouldn't go far, and that should Ashmere ever seek him in earnest, he could be found. I know this all happened before any of us in this room were born, but we all know he existed, if just by the stories we were all raised on. That's not even to mention the dreams he left behind, so that all of us might see the giant in red in our sleep and know that we can still find him should we ever need to look.

"Now the door in the mountain isn't something entirely new, for I remember some small mention of it in my childhood. But it's clearly something that's been forgotten—almost so quickly and entirely as to suggest it was deliberately removed from the tales we tell."

One of the many shadowy strangers stood to speak. "What if the door never stuck as well to the story because it was added later? I never thought it was real myself—how could it be?"

Another cut in. "But what of the Circle of Scholars? Not only are they finding evidence that the door was real, they're saying it was used long before Lord Titus."

"Ashmere is a land of many mysteries, gentlemen," said Hector, "and the door is but one of them. I may not know all the answers but I do know two things: first, that Lord Titus promised we could find him should we need him, and second, that the Circle of Scholars is close to finding the door through which he left. If we can find the door, we can appeal to Lord Titus to set things right with the appointed.

"Concerning the proposition of our new friend here, the Spokesman, I will say only this: it's true that discussion is not against the law. But an organized effort to disrupt the operations of Ashmere *is*. Whereas this search for the door in the mountain constitutes a recovery of our lost history, and is surely of no interest to the chief constable."

"But Hector, where would we start? The Circle

may be able to uncover the door's location, but for now they're still trying to find more evidence that the doors ever existed at all."

"He's right—where would we start on such a search?"

"I'm afraid I don't know either, gentlemen. Perhaps we wait and watch for the Circle's research to progress. To organize a mass strike among the guilds and tradesmen would be treading into treasonous territory, and I dare say such a decision shouldn't be made overnight."

"Let us resolve to wait then and see if we can uncover the door once the Circle has published more findings. Then we take our issue straight to Lord Titus, the one man the appointed will answer to."

When June left the secret gathering that night she was delighted, yet disappointed. She was glad to have heard somewhat from the Circle's research, but it was ultimately the discourse of the night that gripped her to the core. In her short twenty years of life she had never heard such extreme notions as those suggested by the mysterious Spokesman. But just as quickly as it had escalated into ideas of treason, those naysayers that must exist and thrive in every gathering had curtailed the entire affair into utter inaction. And in the end, it was all wasted prattle.

Unlike the tired and bitter men who would congregate in such shaded cellars to discuss the extreme ideas that would never survive if exposed to the light of day, June considered herself a woman driven. And where the Spokesman did not entirely convince her, she found Hector's proposal somewhat more intriguing.

That the door existed was all but certain in June's

mind. Details of Lord Titus's few years in Ashmere had been very thoroughly recorded, from what he built to what he dismantled to what he burned. Though there was the briefest obscure mention of a door through the mountain in the most popular and well-known annals, there was no mention anywhere of Lord Titus destroying the door. In his short time in the hidden country, the Last Lord of Ashmere had dismantled an entire system of government, sank the ships in the bay, burned the docks and even the lighthouse. If he had destroyed the door, the last path to the old world, history would not have forgotten.

Seeing how fervently the appointed fought to silence the Circle of Scholars and keep their research from the public's hands, June suspected the door might be a secret known only to them and kept for decades. But there were still a precious few citizens remaining who lived in and remembered the days of Lord Titus, such as the great Julian. If Ashmere still held such secrets, the country's oldest citizens would know them.

That the door existed was all but without question. The question, ultimately, was whether the citizens of Ashmere could take Lord Titus on his word. And though June was less driven by the thought of being received by Lord Titus on the other side of the mountains, a warmth surged through her.

June knew she would be the one to find the door.

6. THE FIRST MERCHANT
OF ASHMERE

June woke with her wool blanket wrapped around her. It still held the warmth from the small hearth's fire in the front room, now waning in the midmorning's neglect. When the smell of bacon and beans hit her, faint as it was, June jumped from her bed, realizing she had overslept. The long night beneath the library had taken its toll, and she rushed to make up for it. In a matter of moments, she said goodbye to her parents and was on her way.

She had visited five candle-makers the day before, leaving the sixth to be her first stop of the new morning. June found her shop down near the docks overlooking the bay, mere steps from where she and

Duncan often sat together admiring Titus's Grave.
Great Gytha was her name, an aged and entirely
unflappable woman, though not without passion. Like
the other candle-makers, she was already aware of the
tax, and the implications it would have on her. But
unlike the other candle-makers, she held more than
just candles in her shop. At first glance it seemed
chock full of wares, as a general store might, but upon
further inspection June noticed there were only three
wares to choose from: candles, bells, and saddles.

It was a curious selection, June thought, and one in
which she could see no real connection.

Great Gytha was obviously used to such inquiry.
"You see, child, my father was a well-known white
smith in the old world, and people loved him for the
bells he made. He would receive all kinds of orders
from afar and send his works over the sea on the old
ships. He taught me much of the bell craft in my
youth, but very little of other works, and he died of an
old sickness we don't see in Ashmere anymore."

"And what of the saddles?"

"Some time after my father died, my mother
remarried. He was a widower, which I thought was a
good match. Widows and widowers always are, I say.
There's no pretense, no wasted time—only two
people who've already learned not to leave any words
unsaid." She took a long breath. "Anyway, a good
man he was and a gifted leatherworker, eager to teach
me anything I wanted to know. So, I spent the last
half of my youth learning *his* craft."

"Who taught you to make candles?"

"My husband, child. He was a master chandler—
that's what candle-makers used to be called—by the
time he was sixteen. A true talent, he was. So much

that he himself discovered many secrets of the craft. He could make candles that could be used as clocks— have you ever heard of that before?" June shook her head, and the old woman continued. "His clock candles would burn with either green or blue smoke and you could tell when an hour had passed by when the color changed. It was such a marvel. He could even make candles that burned with the scent of ginger or wildflowers."

The old woman's stared at a candle before her, drifting off into distant reverie, but June was much too interested to wait, and instead prompted her again.

"Anyway, I learned much from him, but not all. He never took an apprentice, and many secrets were lost when he died. I appealed to the candle-makers' guild, which is really only a handful of people, and they let me take his place because of their great love for him. He had gone up to make a delivery to the eastern mining camps and decided to ride back to the city through a terrible storm. Anyway, we think he fell asleep in the rain and his horse walked him right off a cliff."

June gasped. "That's terrible. I'm very sorry to hear you've had so much loss in your life."

"Thank you, child, but anyone as old as me has had to watch most of the people she ever knew go before her. What happened to my husband wouldn't have happened in the old world. Things were different then; coin came in and out of the bay and prices were much lower. Back in the old world we would have just paid a carriage to take the load up to the mining camps, but with how the banks have ruined Ashmere there's no way we could afford to do that now."

Through all Great Gytha's stories, June had never considered the old woman's age. If she were so old as to have such varied memories of the old world, then perhaps she might have an answer for June.

"In the days of Lord Titus did you ever hear about his door in the mountain?"

The wrinkled woman frowned as she thought. "I can't say I remember anything of the sort. There were always so many stories going about, even in those days when he was still around. It was hard to know what he did and didn't do."

June had already been too long in staying and steered them back to the matter of the candle taxes. Despite her lengthy stories, Great Gytha's response to the tax was quite simple: she was simply halting the sale of all candles in her store. But because she sold other wares, and she made it especially clear that her bells were more than enough to keep her afloat, she would be less affected than her fellows.

As she left the old woman's shop and walked past Titus's Grave, she took note in her ledger that the city would collect not one farthing of candle taxes for the time being. With exception to Great Gytha, how the candle-makers would survive perplexed June. Any other guild would have paid the tradesmen a stipend while the organization fought the tax—but the candle-makers likely did not have that capacity. Where other guilds consisted of dozens, or even hundreds, of members, the candle-makers were a group of six.

As June made her way across the great square toward the weavers' guild hall, the next item on Cale's list, her mind was occupied further by thoughts of

Great Gytha. She had not intended to inquire after the door until realizing the woman's age, but despite all her stories Great Gytha had nothing to offer on the subject. She may have lived in the era of Lord Titus, but she was not the type who would have rubbed shoulders with him or known his secrets.

It was then that June stopped in the middle of the square, closed the ledger, and placed it back in her satchel. "I'll get to it tomorrow," she said, as explaining to Cale in advance. "I promise."

She turned and marched toward the hall of the Union of Guilds, where the administrators of the Union, including the bookkeepers, held offices. But once inside the hall she did not go to the office of Cale the Counter. She instead found herself standing in the doorway of Julian. He was busy writing in one of the many open books that surrounded him. Among them stood spent candlesticks, early evidence of the Burning Wick's resolve. Not even Julian, the First Merchant of Ashmere, would be spared a light to write by.

As far as legendary figures go, Julian was second only to Lord Titus himself. Normally, this would not have affected June so. She had met him before and knew the old man to be quite approachable, but still there was something about her intended subject that kept her silent as she stood in his doorway. Luckily, he noticed her before long and waved her in to sit across from him.

"I didn't hear you there, young lady. I guess it's true what they say about being old." He winked at her. Something told her he was familiar with the effects of old age long before she was born.

She apologized for bothering him in the middle of

his work and explained her recent graduation into the Union. "You see, Master Julian, when I heard you speak at the ceremony I realized just how little most citizens know about Lord Titus. It's said that you and he rebuilt the city, so I assume you were close with him."

The old merchant pushed away from the table and leaned back in his chair. "We worked well together, yes. He had a vision for Ashmere, and though I don't think I could ever quite comprehend his vision in its entirety, I knew it could only be an improvement to its former state."

"Was Ashmere truly so much worse off before? Just this morning I was talking to a woman who remembered the time before the great war, and I've never heard anyone talk about it the way she did— with such fondness. She actually *misses* the world like it used to be."

"People don't ever miss the world like it used to be, for if things were ever so great they never would have changed. No, Miss Juniper, people miss their youth. They miss the simple way they saw the world when they didn't know it for what it is."

He continued. "There was a time before the great war when our land was the most valuable possession of the old kings who ruled over us from across the south sea. Our mines only produce coal now, but back in those days the miners could almost pick gold right off the mountainside. But not long before Ashmere was summoned to the fight, the king confiscated all the gold in Ashmere's mint to fund his great war. It was a crime, sure, but not the first time the king had simply taken what he wanted.

"After we came back from the war, Lord Titus and

I pleaded with the merchants to pool their gold together to start the First Bank of Ashmere. They were wary at first, as theirs was the largest share of gold taken from the mint just years before, but in the end we convinced them it was the only way for commerce to survive while Ashmere remained hidden. Are you familiar with the bank?"

June shook her head. The bank had no place in the guild system. In fact, for all June had ever heard from her colleagues in the Union, the bank served mainly to frustrate the hidden country's tradesmen.

"Well, with the help of a few of the merchants, we arranged it so that anyone could deposit gold, and in return they'd receive a stamped notice of value, which the bank would exchange for gold at any time. It was they who realized that fortune for all could be made by distributing more notes than gold held in the bank, since they held more gold than would ever be withdrawn at one time."

"But how could that be good for anyone but the banks? It almost sounds like lying."

"You're a bright girl, Miss Juniper, and certainly more used to working with sums than most. But even your most exhaustive training as a bookkeeper has very little equipped you for working with the sums of the bank."

"I ask because lately I've been hearing more and more people talk about the bank. Just in the last day two candle-makers told me they think the bank is ruining the country."

"You know, they call me the First Merchant of Ashmere, but I was the First Banker too, though you'd never hear any of them admit it. It's sad to think that after only two generations the merchants, who were so involved in forming the bank, now stand at odds with it. Most of the guilds share the sentiment, for that matter. But how do you think the candle-maker stays afloat when he's sold all his candles and there's no more tallow left to make more? Most tallow comes from cow fat, you see, and the beefers have a specific season in which they sell their cattle to be slaughtered. That's why there are a few months each year when meat is harder to come by. In those months, tallow is hard to come by too. And the candle-maker, like the rest of us, must wait until the next slaughter to buy more. So, he borrows from the bank against his profit on the candles he's yet to sell."

The old merchant looked slightly irritated, but not with June. "If he's so against the bank, then I suppose he could go back to making candles from beeswax. But there aren't as many beekeepers in Ashmere as there used to be—certainly not enough for a candle-maker to subsist anyway."

"When you look at Ashmere today and see the citizens' discontent and the tension between the guilds and the appointed, do you ever wonder if this was truly the vision Lord Titus had all those years ago?"

"I think his vision extended well beyond our time. If you think of the life of our hidden country as you would a person, then Ashmere is but a babe learning to walk. It may take some time, but eventually she will stand on her own two feet. In his wisdom I think Lord Titus saw beyond that point, to a time when the old world would be safe and Ashmere would be ready to return, even if it be a hundred generations from now."

"Is it true that he'll return at that time?"

"He said such things, yes."

"And do you believe him? Do you think he's still alive out there somewhere?"

His eyes closed gently, and the old man shook his head. "I don't know. I can only say that when I close my eyes I still see him as he was way back when we were the same age as Tinkin." A curious statement, as the messenger in her mind was at least forty years younger than the old merchant sitting before her.

Not wanting to get sidetracked, she shelved the thought in the back of her mind to be discovered again another day. "And what of his door in the mountains?"

"If I ever knew about a door in the mountain, Miss Juniper, I've long forgotten it. I guess it's true what they say about being old," He repeated with another wink.

Her shoulders dropped and she sat back in her own chair. Julian either truly did not remember or he did not want to discuss it. In either case June thought it time to excuse herself.

"Thank you for coming by, Miss Juniper. I don't get to talk about these things very often anymore. It's a marvel how time flies by you. I hope you never find yourself surrounded by hordes of young people who can't understand their privilege because they don't remember how things used to be."

"Thank you for sparing some time to talk with me. I'm always sorry to take any master away from his work."

"You know, I've lived my whole life writing in these ledgers, yet they contain nothing of any value for me anymore. When you're not sure how much time you have left, it's really these conversations that you live for."

She smiled and exited into the dark stone hall, but before she got far he called to her.

"If you want to know more about Lord Titus, there may be a better person to ask than me. She was truly close to him, where I mostly worked alongside him. She used to live in the western reaches of the city, and last I heard she was still alive. She used to be the finest glass-maker in Titus Bay—her name was Mira."

7. A VISIT WITH OLD MIRA

Though June had spoken with the old merchant for only a few minutes, the exchange felt like it had taken hours, and she was surprised to find the sun at its highest peak when she finally left the Union hall. Next on Cale's list was a weaver near the center of the city, and though she knew the routine, she knew neither her heart nor mind would be in her work for the rest of that day. The old merchant had ruined her. Cale the Counter would not have his assistant back in her fullest capacity until she spoke to Mira.

Luckily for June, Cale was gone, and though she would never shirk her duties, his absence allowed for some room for her mind to be elsewhere while she visited with the weaver. He was a young man, only recently advanced from his journeymanship. After his years wandering between the mining camps, farmers, and cattle-herders, he had finally received full admittance into the weavers' guild as a master and had returned home to work with his aging father. His father having already worked for decades in his quaint little shop near the city center, the new weaver was already better established than most of his peers, and after only a couple hours June found him to have his books in order.

Though many in Titus Bay referred to the two Union bookkeepers as tax collectors, it was a mere misconception. In truth, Cale and June collected no taxes whatsoever. The Union, mistaken by many to be a government entity that served the appointed, was in reality created to act as a bridge between the guilds and the appointed. Essentially a guild made up of other guilds, the Union was responsible for the general oversight of its members—as any normal guild was responsible for its members. The Union therefore took an accounting of the production of each guild, using its own audits to verify and calculate proper taxes.

Not understanding that he would pay city tax collectors and surveyors, true agents of the appointed, the young weaver had come prepared to pay his taxes directly to June. And while the weaver had borne her no ill will, June's audits and visits were met with an air of resentment. But it was all groundless—the product of confusion too proud to learn.

If so many guildmasters could get the wrong impression of the Union, which was such an involved part of their life as tradesmen, then perhaps they also misunderstood the actions of the bank, as Julian said.

People are so often more wont to misunderstand than to understand, for who can teach a person something contrary to what they already know? June had certainly never seen it done.

These thoughts were, of course, but a brief aside to those of Mira that she was anxious to tend to, and as she left the young weaver she walked with all the fervency of the fire brigade called to action, not that she had ever seen such a sight. Regardless, the close of the day was near enough that she put her list away and headed for the library. She knew Duncan would be as enraptured by the news as she.

With that supposition driving her hastened steps toward the library, she nearly tripped at his response to her revelation. "Well of course Mira knew Lord Titus. We've always known that—don't you remember the story?"

"What story?"

"It was about how Mira was the chief glass-maker in her time, but for some reason woke up one day and remembered nothing. As the story went, she sought the wisdom of Lord Titus and he told her to swim in the pools of the Sylvain, and when she emerged from the water she could remember again. I think I first heard it from the other children in our lessons, but even these days the glass-makers love the story."

She looked around west wing, empty and dark in the late afternoon sun. "Then lock up and we'll be off. We should go talk to her at once."

"June, the old woman's mind isn't straight anymore. She's been alone too long. She whispers to herself and only comes outside to tend her garden. You know this as well as I."

"It may take years for the Circle of Scholars to find

clues enough to lead to the door. I want to find it, Dun, and I'm not one to wait at the mercy of others. Old Mira may be the only person left who ever knew where the door was."

Duncan admitted that he too was very curious about the door and had been quite disappointed by the east wing's resolve of inaction the night before. With the library closed, June helped him finish his duties tidying up, straightening shelves, and returning books to their proper place. In those days of Ashmere, the library was not so much a luxury of the common citizens as it was a repository of knowledge for those professionals and tradesmen whose breadth of field was so wide as to warrant research as it was needed. Be it barber-surgeons and apothecaries searching for forgotten treatments for various ailments or city planners looking through ancient annals, the bells of the library were more often rung for the purposes of research than recreation. As such, it was all but impossible to deduce the identity of the Circle of Scholars by someone's presence in the library.

June would leave the research to the Circle. She and Duncan would take another path to the same destination, albeit one hopefully much more direct.

Their shadows followed them as they wove their way through the crowd of men and women toward the west highway. Behind the east wing the merchant vendors of the central square could be heard closing up shop, a scene distinguishable by the sound of hooves upon the cobblestone. Horses, while not unheard of, were something of a rare sight in Titus Bay, as the laws of the city permitted horses in the street only when pulling a cart or on the city's errand.

Nearby, at the northeast corner of the square were the city stables. The space had originally been designated for the use of horses owned by city officers, but many of the larger merchant vendors were more than willing to pay to have their horses boarded each day while they worked in the square. With the close of day, they were retrieving their animals and pulling their carts home for the night.

Along the east highway, June and Duncan stayed off to the side as they walked, careful not to get in the way of the passing carts and the massive beasts pulling them. At a certain corner, they passed a messenger post where the citizens attached letters to be delivered. As infrequent and unpredictable as the Circle of Scholars was in publishing their research, they had always nailed it to the countless posts standing throughout the city—likely for the simple reason that the posts offered the best chance of being seen by the most citizens.

Her eyes quickly searched the folded papers pinned to the wood as she passed, before she remembered the time of day. Even if there had been something published that day, it would have been pulled down from every post in the city by midday.

As they went further and further away from the center of the city, the traffic dwindled and houses grew further apart, separated by small arms of the forest that still reached outward toward the highway. Past her own home, June could see the shape of the old woman's cottage through the shadows of the trees. Tucked back deeper into the forest than the other cottages, Mira's was so mossy and overgrown that it looked a part of the woods itself. The thatch of the roof was covered in leaves of the taller trees, green and rotting in the wet shade of the evening, and vines had climbed the side, breaking in and out of the wattle as it grew. The only break in the overgrown vines was the firewood stacked and leaning against the stone chimney. June had never noticed the firewood before, and had certainly never noticed anyone delivering it.

The house was still standing, of course, and as such it fulfilled its first purpose in providing shelter. But its condition showed its age as much as the woman who lived in it.

As they tread over the tall grass that had grown through the stone walkway, June turned to Duncan. "When I was young my mother would send Tansy and I over with porridge at the end of each week. We would always knock once and then let ourselves in. Old Mira doesn't answer her door very quickly, but mother always thought it polite to at least announce our coming."

Following her childhood directions, June gave a loud rap on the door and pushed it ajar. "Good evening, madam," she called out into the shuttered darkness inside. "It's Juniper Gladwell from next door come to visit you. Are you awake?"

"I am," answered a small and shivering voice. "Come around, dear."

As humble as it was on the outside, the cottage was quite spacious within and, from the distance of the voice answering her in the dark, it extended further into the forest than was visible from the road. Duncan grabbed June's hand as she stepped forward into the dark, feeling for the wall before her. A faint light could be seen off to the side, and they followed the wall until a deep hearth room came into view.

Seated before the smoldering fire was the same old woman June had known all her life. For a moment June felt a twinge of guilt run through her, for she had never shown much interest in Mira before. But now the old woman was a character of great mystery, and June could not have been more captivated by anyone else in the entire country. In that moment, even Duncan came second.

The old woman sat comfortably in a cushioned chair, where June supposed she likely slept. June sat in an old wooden chair across from her while Duncan tossed another log on the fire. Mira looked at him and nodded, a silent gratitude that only the elderly, in their struggle to maintain their speech, can get away with.

"You have a lovely home. Do you get many visitors?"

Though Mira's eyes had met them initially when they walked into view, they now stared into the fire, empty and unaware. Her head shook ever so slightly, and June took that for her answer.

"We thought we would come visit you today to learn about your life. You knew Lord Titus, didn't you? Is it true he told you to swim in the pools of the Sylvain as the stories say?"

A long moment passed as those old eyes gazed into the burgeoning flames, and June was about to ask another question when those old lips finally spoke. "It wasn't just me. We *both* swam. The pools weren't so revered in those days. It was a place for young lovers, you see. Not like today."

"What was he like, Lord Titus?"

"I don't know." She turned to them and fidgeted in her seat, as if the very words she spoke brought some small measure of life to the woman. "It's hard to speak of a man like Titus, who won not only my heart but the hearts of our entire country. And even though I've thought of him every day since, I know I had more time with him than most, and if I never do see him again I'll always be grateful for that."

"Do you remember where he went? Do you remember how he left Ashmere?"

Old Mira nodded.

June and Duncan both leaned toward her, eager for more, yet barely able to contain the questions. "Do you know where the door is? Did you ever see it?"

"Oh, yes. But it's been so long I don't think I could ever find it again."

By now it seemed to June that the woman, in the course of speaking, had grown twenty years younger. She spoke of Lord Titus with a passion met only by the fire now raging in the hearth before her. Both June and Duncan sat back in their chairs, ready for a lengthy visit. Seeing what this talk of Lord Titus did to rejuvenate the old woman, June was confident they could jog her memory, and so they told her of the Circle of Scholars and their quest to find the door.

"They weren't of his making. As far as I remember the doors were around long before Titus or even Ashmere." An assertion not altogether surprising to June, yet one detail of the old woman's speech bothered her until she felt compelled to ask.

"Why do you say *doors*?"

"Because, dear, there were two."

8. FINDING NETTLEROOT

"I only ever saw the door through the eastern mountains, you see, though Titus did on occasion speak of the other in the west. Perhaps his great advantage was that he knew the location of both. You know, he actually came and went many times without the citizens even knowing he was gone. Most of them didn't know the doors existed at all, but even so, when Titus went through the mountain he would always lock the door from the inside to keep anyone from wandering beyond the hidden country and alerting anyone to our existence."

Mira spoke slowly, and as she spoke a slight movement in the darkness caught June's eye. Just behind the old woman, just beyond the light of the hearth, June could see a cat perched atop a bookshelf. Its tail waved about slowly, bouncing like a reed in the wind, and June watched the fire dance in its eyes as it watched them with no small interest.

"If you knew where he came and went, why didn't you go with him when he left for the final time?"

"It's easy to fall in love with a man," she said, her eyes darting from June to Duncan and back, "as you well know, young lady, but Titus was at the same time so much more than just a man. It's a strange thought to claim something that so clearly belongs to everyone, and though he *did* ask me to come join him when I was ready, I was afraid to leave my life behind for whatever he found beyond the mountains. For years I stayed, scared to never see my parents and family again, until one day I woke up with nothing to fear, for they had all passed away. By the time I worked up the courage to go I was already an old woman and had long forgotten the way. I spent years looking, but to no avail."

June had always heard that Mira, in her younger days, had been a renowned woman of nature and spent much of her time in the forest. But she was likely no lover of nature at all. All that time people had noticed her absence, all those years she spent out in the trees—Mira had been secretly searching for the door.

June was lost in that thought when she was brought back into the moment by Duncan's voice. "Do you remember anything that may be of use in our search for it?"

"He was a great lover of music, Titus, and he built an amphitheater and assembled a band to help pass his love on to others. But time has passed and the country has forgotten the amphitheater. When he left it was as if most of the music went with him. That's what happens when you lose someone you love, and I think all of Ashmere hurt as much as I when he left."

The old woman caught her digression, beginning anew in a louder voice. "In those days, Titus Bay wasn't the only town in Ashmere. There used to be a small town in the foothills, built in the forest around a great myrtle tree. This was before the mining camps moved, mind you, and Titus had built the amphitheater to be a relief for the miners.

"The miners ended up moving their town north a few years after he left, so I doubt much sign of it still remains. Though I lost the way long ago, I do think I could find my way to the door if I ever saw the myrtle again."

As the fire again smoldered, June looked behind her to the closed shutter and realized it was dark outside. The feline form atop the bookshelf was lost in the darkness, with only its eyes still revealing its presence. The old woman had not said much, but the speed in which she said it had consumed the evening. Standing to leave, the pair thanked Mira for allowing them in her home, and promised to return should they find anything.

The next morning brought a grand excitement to Titus Bay, as the messenger posts bore a newly-printed page from the Circle of Scholars. And whereas under any other circumstance June would have been quite eager to read it, she had ever so silently declared that she would be the one to find the door. As she went about her business that day, checking off the items left to her by Cale, she resisted the Circle's draw, for her pride would not let her read it.

And though June knew not what the publication said, its revelation was evidently quite compelling. As if she were Ashmere's last beekeeper, she heard droves of citizens buzzing about the city, preparing to journey beyond the city to scour the eastern foothills for the fabled door. Perhaps more citizens shared Hector's dream of finding Lord Titus at the door than the librarian possibly knew. What else could drive so many to go off in such blind pursuit? This was not a short trip, by any means. It was nearly a full day's ride up to the foothills of the hidden country's eastern reach—and even longer on foot.

Seeking some measure of respite from the zeal floating throughout the city, June stopped into the library to see Duncan. He was already well aware of the new research, and could see the anxiety building in her.

"You're afraid someone else will find it first, aren't you?"

"Well aren't you? Perhaps we should take two horses and ride east tonight." As Union administration, the bookkeepers enjoyed access to the horses in the city stables, a privilege to which Cale the Counter helped himself, though June rarely partook.

"I've got an idea, but—" he hesitated.

"What is it?"

"The chief constable's here."

"What do you mean? He's in the library at midday?"

"He's here quite often actually, but I don't know what he's doing."

Chains hung from both sides of the narrow aisle, and as Duncan led her down she noticed just how many chains hung freely over empty shelf space, the books that once occupied it removed long ago. Whether their absence was the result of theft or ancient oppression was unclear, though Duncan had on numerous occasion voiced suspicion of the latter. But for the first time, and though June never would have said it aloud to Duncan or Hector, she saw that the library was in a state of deep disrepair.

Past rows and rows they walked until they finally came to a long table given light by an open window high above. Three open books lay on the end of the table, and the chief constable sat hunched before them, his hands scribbling upon a small paper.

They made it uncomfortably close without his notice. June, wanting to not scare the man, said, "Uncle Ly, what are you doing here?"

"Juniper!" He sat up startled despite her calm tone. "Come away from your work to check on me, eh? There are dark whispers about the city, June, and my deputies and I have our hands full with an investigation. I can't say too much about it yet, you understand, but suffice it to say I've come here to clear my head. Sometimes you can't see the forest for the trees, and sometimes you don't know the questions you should be asking for all the answers right before you. I find that writing brings clarity of vision. And what better place to write than here?"

She knew the chief constable to write in his spare time, and could see now that before him were laid dictionaries and word lists. His was a unique soul in Ashmere, restless and always stirring his heart to new endeavors. Simply being the chief constable was not enough for him.

"What are you working on now?"

"Just a little piece on the Vision of Titus." That Lord Titus had left some spell on the citizens of Ashmere to cause them to share the same dream was an acknowledged fact by all, but very few spoke openly about it. Of all he left behind, the legacy that might one day decay just as the once grand library, that immortal dream that manifested to every citizen, and to some more often than others, could nurture their memory of him and his promises.

Seeing more of her uncle than usual, June asked to read his work, and though he was hesitant to let anyone see the verse too soon, he lifted the paper and held it up in the light for her.

Did you hear in the wood the grand parade
Whose harmony hailed from some secret glade,
Where the conductor in crimson leads the band
Under weeping willows and dappled shade?

Over the hills and through the briar,
I came to the sound of sweet lute and lyre,
The great conductor took me hand in hand,
To sing the wistful tune of wildfire.

But as I turned and began to sway,
And the band dissolved and the sprites ran away,
The conductor alone was left to stand,
And the willows gloated their part in the play.

Reading the verse, June could not help but nod, for the Vision of Titus was truly just as described. It was impossible to know exactly the dreams of others, of course, but she could remember in her youth how the other children would describe the dreams. They were anything but articulate, as so very few children are, but all seemed to describe the same scene: a merry band marching across a grass stage and then deep into the woods. They would eventually disappear as they rounded a tree, never to be seen on the other side.

She lowered the paper from the pillar of light and returned it. "It's very good, Uncle Ly."

"The problem is I can't tell if it's finished. The Vision is such an oddity—I feel like there's more to say than my words here have said."

"Maybe it's less about what your words say and more about what your words can make others say."

"Perhaps I'll turn it into a song." He smiled, his wispy mustache curling upward. "It's been so long since a song was written in Ashmere, although I don't know how to play." He stared at the paper, instantly as lost in thought as June had just been. After a moment, he came back into the room with a jerk and looked up at the pair before him. "What are you doing here, anyway?"

Both June and Duncan hesitated, their eyes meeting in the silence.

"We've been a little intrigued by the Circle of Scholars' research and thought we'd come look through some of the annals in our free time to compare to what they're publishing." After the severity of words spoken at the gathering beneath the east wing, she knew better than to mention it, for her involvement in such underhanded dealings, whether she was fervent for the cause or not, would surely break the man's heart.

To her surprise, he simply grinned and rolled his eyes. "Well don't get too deep into looking or you're bound to never find your way out of this maze of books. It's all nonsense, you know. But with all the rumors of secret rebellion driving my investigation, I'm glad the Circle of Scholars is at least serving to distract some of the more boisterous citizens from their discontent."

She had not expected such a response and was glad the chief constable had not inquired further. Otherwise, June might have had to lie. There was no need to worry him, and if he knew she was present in any sort of gathering where citizens were discussing rebellion, that is precisely what he would do. Had the group settled on some treasonous action, she might have been more tempted to inform him. But as doing so would implicate Hector, she was glad the rowdy group had chosen inaction in the end. It saved her from any truly hard choices.

The city annals were kept in the south wing of the library. Such records were open to the common citizen, of course, but from the look of the dust that coated everything in sight, June could see, as Duncan told her, that it was the least visited area of the library. Its disuse puzzled June, for her first and natural thought was that the south wing was the source of the Circle's research.

But despite the sprawling decay of its ever-emptying shelves, the library still held many, many books. Perhaps there were still histories and records even Hector and Duncan did not know about.

Duncan knew roughly the area that would serve their needs, and he pulled volume after volume out onto a nearby table.

"Here are ten years of every city record up until the time of Lord Titus's departure. Back then the old city historians recorded everything of public interest in the city—from the weekly city council gatherings to festivals. So, if Lord Titus's amphitheater hosted the citizens to hear the band play, it'll surely be in here. We'll have to hope the historians recorded its locations.

The afternoon passed as the two of them sat in silence, searching through the volumes for any sign of the amphitheater. June could not help but feel she had wasted the day on her vain search, and by the time the light of the windows had left the floor and climbed high on the stone walls, even Duncan seemed frustrated by their fruitless endeavor. As Duncan closed the volume before him and slumped back in defeat, June's eyes moved faster and faster over the dimming text, and she flipped pages quickly for anything that caught her eye.

Duncan was up and replacing the books upon the shelves when June broke the hours long silence. "Duncan, I think I've found something." He dumped his armload upon a shelf, rushing over to see where she held her finger over the text. "It mentions grand concerts at the *Nettleroot Theater.* Apparently at the time of the concerts, Lord Titus and his appointed attendants would formally leave the city to ride for the theater, and a procession of citizens would follow. They did this many times, as Lord Titus wanted every citizen to see it at least once. But it doesn't say where the theater is."

Telling her to wait a moment, Duncan disappeared into the maze of darkness. He emerged before long, lit by a hefty candle and several papers rolled under his arm. With candle giving light to the table once again, he spread the papers out. Each was a map of

Ashmere.

"Our whole country was once called Sylvain. It was back before there was any open land for crops and cattle, and it was all woodland. But once we pushed the forest outward, the Sylvain simply surrounded us. Now the tree-cutters are replacing the trees of the old forest with their spongy oak and the name is shifting again to the river that finds it source in the woods' northern reaches. But Nettleroot is another name I've seen in some of the old books."

Above one of the maps he pointed to the foothills. "Just as Ashmere is surrounded by the Sylvain, the forest itself is surrounded by the Nettleroot, the thick brush of the foothills. The tree-cutters keep the undergrowth at bay these days, but back then the Nettleroot had much more territory than it does now. And," he grabbed the volume June had been reading, "this entry and this map were made in the same year—"

June cut him off. "What if Nettleroot was the name of the town Mira spoke of?"

"Just what I was thinking—and look here." He pointed down to the old map. There was a strange symbol drawn deep in the forest-laden foothills, marks that could, with an open mind and squinted eyes, resemble the silhouette of many roofs against the sky. "The *Nettleroot* written here is probably referring to the town rather than the forest."

"And since Mira said the mining town was close by the amphitheater, we can probably find it if we follow this map to the symbol. Whether it's the amphitheater or the town, if we find one we should be able to wander into the other."

He rolled up the map and looked down at her, the

candle lighting his eyes. "Now that we have this, when do we leave?"

Up until then, June had felt herself the driving force of their search. There was no real reason compelling her—just curiosity. And until then Duncan had been simply indulging her. But now he looked as enamored as she, and June could not help but throw her arms around his neck.

"I'll get the horses," she whispered.

9. A NIGHT ON THE NORTHEAST HIGHWAY

Though at least one stable hand was always present to watch over the horses in the night, June knew them to be an especially sleepy lot. It was the rigors of working with obstinate beasts that did them in, and as June entered the stables she heard snoring coming from the small enclosed quarters at the row's end. It mattered not to her, for she was well within her right as a Union official to fetch horses at any time. Whether she was on the city's errand was another question entirely, but one sleeping stable boy could not ask.

The end of the third row housed the city's many horses, and as June turned to follow the open aisle back she stopped at a beast that always drew her interest. He was a beautiful creature, white but speckled with the color of a yearling stag, and looked to possess a strength that would rival an ox. There was not another horse in Ashmere half as wondrous in the city, and June often wondered if his owner truly knew the treasure he had.

In the eastern reaches of Titus Bay, where the hilly terrain of the city begins to level out to the plain, lie the estates of the appointed and Ashmere's wealthiest. Among them lived Heward Wesgold, the richest baker in the city. He had made his fortune serving those who would later count him amongst their ranks, and in the process, had acquired the finer tastes and hobbies that abound in high society—including horses. Though he rode the single stallion long and often, he was the type of man not to be bothered with the menial upkeep related to owning such a beast, and paid well for the space and service of the stables. June was well assured of the beast's power, for she had watched over the years as the baker's portly frame formed the poor colt into a steed of such strength that no workhorse in the grainlands could match its great endurance.

In the briefest flash of sinister thoughts, June considered taking the stallion, for in all the years she had known the horse she had not once ridden him. But knowing they would not return before morning, she decided against it, for the freshly-awakened stable hand would surely notice. Instead she bid the animal farewell and rushed off to fetch two of the city's horses and met Duncan in the empty square.

Just beyond the city, the cobblestone of the northeast highway gradually turned to dirt, deep-rutted and scarred by the wheels of countless carts pulled to and from the foothills in decades long past. They were the miners', no doubt, and from the look of the ruts, heavy laden with the plunder of the mountain.

It was an anxious autumn night that welcomed them, cold and foreboding of impending winter. The moon illuminated their way with a pale glow, and, every once in a while, the night's light revealed the presence of a familiar feline follower, his tail still caught in that peculiar bounce that hinted at a wind that was not there. From the look of his longer fur, June could now see he was a forest cat and she wished it would sit in her lap so she could warm her hands. She turned around in her saddle to call the animal closer, but found him gone, off to find some field mouse, perhaps. Turning forward again, she blew into her frozen fists and tucked them deep into her cloak, resigned to the next few hours of cold. It was a familiar punishment for one so given to impulse as June.

In their rush to leave the city, neither June nor Duncan had given thought to bringing with them what many would consider necessary for an overnight trek deep into the forest. Having left straight from the library, Duncan only took a small lantern. It did them no service in the face of the bold moon, but the pair willed the flame on in hopes of using it to soon start a fire and warm themselves. The horses walked slow, but otherwise showed no sign of being bothered by the night's frigid air, and though they would make the trip at least twice as fast, June found herself wishing they had walked so she and Duncan might walk in one another's arms and find warmth.

As they rode the two lovers passed the time speaking of life and the goings on of Titus Bay. Every so often Duncan would unfurl the map and hold it to catch the moonlight just so. It was ornately decorated with much attention given to the highways and smaller roads of Ashmere, but left much to be desired when it came to distances. It was a cramped little country they lived in, but this old map, perhaps drawn in an early era of fervor and optimism, seemed to emphasize the vast space between destinations— room that June suspected was not there. Duncan shared her concern as well, and since many of the paths leading from the highway out to the place of the old mining camp had not been used in many decades, he was nervous lest they pass it unknowingly.

Duncan's path reached out to the highway much earlier than June expected, and before long they found themselves deep in the forest. No longer was their way open and illuminated for them. Instead, mottled moonlight danced across the path, bearing the same wheel marks of the highway but also long overgrown so as to hide the age-old scars.

When hours more had passed and the little lamp could no longer give enough light to consult the map, they stopped to make camp. They knew they were close, but no amount of wandering in the darkness would bring them any closer to the door, and so they decided to sleep until dawn. Duncan rushed to gather wood and, with the lantern's last breath, passed the withering flame from the lamp to the makeshift campfire.

Sat finally on the ground, hugging her cloak tightly, June leaned forward toward the warmth. Duncan wrapped his own cloak around her shoulders and stepped even closer, his eyes closed in some ineffable contentment. After taking new life from the heat, he sat down next to her.

"You've gotten my hopes up, you know."

"That we'll find the door?"

"That perhaps all isn't lost for us citizens. That we don't have to just lie down and die. We can go after the things we want. We can chase our ambitions and fight our fears. Do you know what my greatest fear is, June?"

She shook her head.

"I think my greatest fear is to be forgotten. Ashmere forces every citizen to play their part, but in the end, they're all lost to time and memory. And I'm afraid that unless something changes soon, I'm going to be just like them. I'll have nothing to show for my time here—it will all be in vain. But I want more than that. I want to leave something behind, something great for people to remember me by."

"I think perhaps the time of legacies are over. But what should that have to do with you? Surely everyone leaves their mark on this world in one way or the other—even if they never live to realize it."

Duncan shook his head. "We'd have seen more change by now. Sixty years we've been living under the heel of the appointed, and from the sound of it things are just as they were then. No, Lord Titus was the last one to truly make his mark, and in all the years since we haven't been allowed to forget it."

They had lain down under their cloaks, staring up at the hardiest stars whose light fought their way through the branches. June did not break her upward gaze, but she knew tears were streaming down the face of her Duncan. After a moment, he took her hand under the warm cover of the cloak. "But if Lord Titus *is* out there still at the end of some tunnel leading through the mountain, then perhaps we still have reason to hope."

10. THE VISION
OF TITUS

In the morning, they awoke and found themselves
not far from the place of the old mining town. June
had been unsure what they would find there, or if
they would even recognize it, as it had been
abandoned so long before. But just at the base of the
foothill's incline a broad clearing still remained,
though the trees were heavily encroaching.

A few brittle structures still stood scattered about
and a few flat stones paced the distance between
them, remnants of the town's streets now upended by
rain and root. Between the not-so-ancient ruins of the
town were littered all manner of rubbish. The grass,
up to June's knees, hid most signs of waste, and the

pair walked their horses further along the overgrown road.

Duncan pointed to a splintered barrel off to the side of their path. "The miners have always been a rowdy bunch, and even back then they loved their drink. The bee-keepers used to make a special wine from their honey. It was held in barrels like this."

"How do you know such things?"

"I read it in a book somewhere." He gave the question little thought, instead pulling out the map once again. He announced that another road should meet theirs in the town and lead up into the foothills to the amphitheater. Overgrown as it was, the old stone roads throughout the ruins were scarcely noticeable, and it was not long before the two had separated to cover more ground in their search.

As they wandered in circles in and out of the tree line, June grew impatient and called out to Duncan, "If the road we want leads into the foothills, can we not just head into the foothills? Surely we'll happen upon the amphitheater."

"The problem is everything east of us at this point are the foothills, and they reach down from the mountains like great fingers upon the land below. Going up a path to the wrong ridge could render us completely blind to what may lie on the other side. But don't worry, dear Juniper," he shouted through the trees, and she could hear the smile on his face, "I think I've found it now."

What he found could hardly have been described as a path, but when June looked at it just right she could see how the older, larger trees hinted at a path obscured by younger growth below. The woods once again grew thicker and thicker, though the path maintained what little surety they had given in the first place.

As dark and dense as the forests of Ashmere could be, they were not dangerous, and the sounds of late autumn could still be heard through the shivering branches. She could hear geese flying south high above the treetops, and as she looked around she noticed squirrels traipsing up and down the trees. It was likely that no citizen had tread that lost path since the days of Lord Titus, and despite their absence the forest had gone on living.

June was taken from her thoughts by Duncan, who pointed out two large posts standing bestride the path ahead of them. From one hung an enormous sheet of dirty linen.

"It looks like a banner," June said. They rode between the posts, and the path rounded to reveal stone benches that climbed the steep hill, row after row. Many of the benches were either broken or hidden by the grass and growth that had overtaken the hill. At their base was a small glade separating them from a large and abrupt grassy step.

"It's the stage," June said.

"We're here, then," said Duncan. "We found it."

They walked about the place for some time, marveling at the size of it. June had never heard of such a grand thing being built in Ashmere, and for all the work that it must have taken, she could not understand how it could have been forgotten. If the foothills were truly a hand sprawling down from the mountains, the amphitheater was nestled right behind a curled thumb. The walls about the place were steep, leaving little space to explore in search of Mira's myrtle tree.

The only place to look, then, was up above.

But they found the forest above to be just as dense as below, and the two left their horses to graze near the stage below while they resumed their separate searches. As she wandered aimlessly through the growth, June watched the sun crawl its way across the sky, peeking in through sparse breaks in the branches overhead.

It was a precarious search, of course, as June had never seen a myrtle before in her life. She wandered down the hill again, hoping by chance that something out of place might catch her eye, some tree recognizable by its incredible height or colored blossoms. But she only saw green.

At the bottom, she again met Duncan, who had taken an even wider route down the hill. June could see his frustration in his composure, in the very way he was walking.

"This has taken too long already." He shook his head. "Even if we leave now we won't make it back to Titus Bay by nightfall."

They sat on the lowest bench, and June leaned into his chest and stroked his hair. "It's alright if we don't find it, Dun. We have time. We found this place once, and it'll still be here when we come back. Maybe Mira could find the door from here."

"Everyone wants to sit about and wait for things to happen, but I want to make things happen. You want to make things happen too, June, you always have. That's something I love about you. Why are you so content now to turn around and ride home without finding what we came here for?"

"A few months ago, we hadn't even heard of the door. We certainly didn't know where it was, so if this journey proves unfruitful, how much can we truly despair? Nothing has changed. We'll find it next time."

"There may not be a next time. The appointed grow bolder by the day. It's just a matter of time before they uncover the Circle of Scholars and they outlaw any search for the door. Before long we won't even be able to mention the door, and everyone will forget again. Just like all the books they've taken from the library." Sitting with him in her arms, June could tell he was not only not calming down, but quite the opposite. As if finishing a conversation with himself, he shook his head and stood. He ambled the way they had come, his head low and defeated, saying, "When that man spoke of rebellion the other night under the east wing, I knew in my heart he was right. Even if Lord Titus *did* promise to come back, he's long dead now. Meanwhile his people search for him in the woods rather than standing up to the appointed."

She rose to follow him, but stopped herself at the gate. He was rarely ever so emotional, but she could tell his problem was not for her to fix—at least not in that moment. Just as all steaming kettles cool, so too did Duncan need some time to himself. As he disappeared into the trees, she turned again to find Mira's cat sitting on the front row where she had just been. His tail still waved in that silent, imperceptible breeze, but he did not move when she retook her place on the bench. In the clear light of day, she could better see his smoky coat, the fur grey at the end and white close to the body. It was a curious color that looked almost two colors any way she looked at it.

Seemingly unconcerned with her now, the cat let her get close, and he was silent as she ran her hand down his back. He remained motionless, staring forward to the old stage, almost as if expecting something. The stage was but a grassy embankment that rose from the forest floor. Bordered on both sides by great trees, relics of the old forest, it looked to June to be nearly as wide as the broad side of the Union's banquet hall.

She looked down to her new friend. "What are you waiting for, anyway?" She had no way of knowing how old the cat was, but if he was Mira's, then perhaps it had been to the place before and remembered the performance. But that would make it over sixty years old, and June had never heard of a sixty-year-old cat before. But still, she could not help but wonder what held his gaze.

June joined the feline in his listless gaze forward, trying to imagine what grand concerts were held there back in the days of Lord Titus. She could almost hear the faintest of notes ringing through the trees, music long forgotten to all but the sleeping ears of Ashmere. She closed her eyes and heard the tune more clearly, an ensemble of lutes, trumpets, bells, and more with sounds so sweet she could taste them as she listened.

When something finally stirred her from her long reverie, she looked down to see the cat still sitting beside her, but his ears were twitching, almost as if to the beating of the drums. The music had not stopped. It was louder than ever and quite unmistakably not her imagination, and June gasped for breath when she saw the long procession crossing the stage.

The conductor led them in a formation that June thought best described as a parade. He was a great tall man, dressed in deep red accoutrements with shining gold trim about the chest and epaulets. At the center stage he stepped out of formation to stand opposite June, and he marched in place to the rhythm while the band danced and played their merry way across, disappearing behind the great tree to the right.

It was the Vision of Titus. But at the same time, it was so clearly not quite the same vision she had come to know. The scene was all wrong. There was always a great tree the parade disappeared behind, but it was certainly not at the end of a stage before an amphitheater.

The tune came to her mind as easily as a lullaby, those sweet hushed notes sung of a mother's voice which children never truly forget. But the scene before June played like a sweet lullaby sung by a stranger. Yet it was no stranger. June recognized the conductor, down to his thin mustache, as the man who led the parade in her dreams. It was the visage of Lord Titus. She grappled with the thought and pinched herself twice to make sure she was truly awake.

As the last of the procession left the stage, the conductor fell in line behind them and followed their footsteps off the stage and out of sight behind the tree, stopping only for a moment to wave June to follow. The cat was already on the stage by the time June rose from her seat, stumbling to catch up.

Behind the tree the proceeding troupe had turned sharply away from the amphitheater and was marching downhill. As all but the conductor seemed unaware of both her presence and the fact that there was no audience watching, June walked wide to watch them better. The forest was thick and dark except where they passed, for the forest seemed to clear a way for them, and each member of the merry band

92

glowed as with the light of the full moon.

Soon enough the light of the band grew dim, and June looked forward to the head of the parade to see members disappearing behind something in the dark. The music grew weaker and weaker as each member vanished in the darkness, and when the great conductor in red joined his band behind the unknown June found herself humming their sweet tune to keep herself from forgetting.

With the parade gone the forest once again moved and swayed with its own life, and with the light now penetrating through the tops of the trees, June could now see what it was the troupe had rounded into oblivion. It was a giant, twisted mess of roots and trunks weaving their way sideways instead of upward; it was Mira's lost myrtle.

11. SPEECHES IN THE CELLAR

It was well into the early night when the far reaches of Titus Bay came into view, and June and Duncan rode toward the city gates in silence. The moon had not yet shown its face, and in the still air June could see darkness peeking out through the slats of closed shutters where no candles burned within. She imagined the great manors of the appointed, as dark and still as these common citizens in the farthest reaches of the city. The chief constable had rolled his eyes at the candle-makers' obstinate statement, but as June surveyed the mass darkness she had to admit she heard them loud and clear.

Or perhaps she simply hoped they were being

heard. The Spokesman had spoken of more drastic measures to be taken, but if these efforts were successful in changing the minds of the appointed, then no mass strike among the guilds would be necessary.

Like a dry leaf in the autumn breeze, Duncan was blowing to and fro on the matter, but still seemed to be floating closer and closer to the Spokesman's philosophy. Even after June's discovery of the myrtle tree, he seemed aloof and unaffected. She thought back over his words concerning the books of the library, the knowledge of the old world that was, at some point or another, curated by an unknown authority and removed. Though she had not heard him speak of it thus, he had never been so close to inheriting Hector's position. And as he fast approached the title he would likely hold for the rest of his life, she mused, perhaps he was seeing the same hand of irreproachable authority interfering in the lives of the common citizens.

He was passionate, she knew. He always had been, and about a great many things. But as she looked across to the quiet boy riding beside her, she could see that flame of whimsy growing dim. If the myrtle did not encourage him once again, she knew only the door itself would.

By the time they returned the horses to the stables the moon was out in full force. They still had not spoken more than a few words since entering the city, but Duncan insisted on walking her home.

"I'm sorry, June. I want to have hope that the door is out there. I want it to be real, and I was willing to march out into the wilderness to prove it was real. But I wonder if we've let the nonsensical words of an old woman steer us further into our own delusion."

"You've always had a gift for looking at others and feeling what they feel. And I think right now you're looking out at your fellow citizens and feeling their discord as your own. We found the myrtle, love. Let's not forget that. And let's certainly not be too quick to follow the Spokesman from our own delusion into his."

"You do know I love you, June?" He leaned down and kissed her. "I'll see this through with you."

He bid her goodnight at her door and headed off in the direction of his own home. She fell asleep that night with no vision of their next steps. But with Cale still beyond the city, June knew she and Duncan had time to figure it out.

After being away from her duties for the whole of two days, June arose the next morning prepared to once again address Cale's list. It was not but a few dozen paces from her door that she heard her name called above the usual morning clamor of the city.

"Miss Juniper! If I may…" The call came from Tinkin, whom she could see weaving his way through the street traffic. Despite her position in the Union, which generally required her to be familiar with most city workers, she had never much needed the service of the messengers. Though she did always enjoy talking to him, she rarely had reason to interact with Tinkin, save for a handful of letters she had received over the years.

"Good morning, sir Tinkin." She greeted him as she would have greeted any acquaintance—warm, but lacking heart. To feign enthusiasm was not always her strongest skill, but she was, after all, a bookkeeper. They were never known for enthusiasm.

"A note for you," he said, holding out a folded piece of paper. She reached into her satchel and paid for the delivery, and the man was back on his way. She watched him scuttle off through the mass of rolling carts and walking citizens and wondered at the efficiency of the man who was hailed as Ashmere's chief messenger. Julian had spoken as if he had once been the same age as Tinkin, yet he looked at least forty years younger. Perhaps it was Tinkin's father the old merchant had spoken of, though June had never heard of him.

She opened the paper and immediately sighed in frustration for having been forced to pay for its delivery. It read:

Juniper Gladwell,
Your presence is requested at the east wing of the city library this evening.

It was, of course, Hector who had sent the message, and though she would have undoubtedly seen him throughout the course of the day, saving her what little money messengers charged for their service, June could read the stress in his words, the tinge of excitement in his writing. His nephew must have told him of Mira and the myrtle tree.

Resolved to not abandon Cale's list completely, June buried her head, trying her best to fight off all thoughts of the door in the mountain, and went to work. As she went about her business, crossing the grand square to and from the Union hall, she resisted a stop by the library, knowing she would surely see Duncan later than night in the cellar below the east wing.

As occupied as she tried to be that day, she made sure not to be late this time. The sun was still peeking over the western mountains when she let herself through the heaving doors that separated the east wing from the great square upon which it bordered. She had beaten even Duncan, and the rest of the secret company, finding only Hector moving slowly about his duties.

He greeted her with a quick smile. "When you told me you were interested in hearing more about the Circle of Scholars, I wouldn't have guessed you'd ever be out wandering the forest for their sake."

"I think it was more for Mira's sake than the Circle's. But things were just as she said; we're only one step away from finding the door."

"That's why I called this gathering tonight, dear— it's quite the development. When Duncan told me I couldn't believe it."

"What do you mean? You're the one who proposed searching for the door in the first place."

"I didn't believe in the door at all, and to be honest I'm still not quite sure what to make of your myrtle. But that Spokesman was proposing treason, and as dissatisfied as I am with the recent happenings of the city, I'm not about to get hanged for playing host to the beginnings of some lunatic's rebellion. No, dear, that was self-preservation at its purest."

"So why have you called a gathering tonight then?"

"To announce what you've found, of course. I may not have thought there was anything to find up in the mountains, but we might as well take advantage of this while we can. At the very least it should serve to sway everyone even further away from any thoughts of treason. I don't expect any strangers to be there, since I only sent for those regulars whom I know."

His reason was sound, but Hector would be proven wrong in only a matter of minutes. One by one, fellows of the secret gathering entered the dark library and shuffled their way toward the cellar. They were familiar at first, and each greeted Hector with a silent nod as they passed. Soon, however, citizens unfamiliar to the librarian stepped through, and Hector looked to June with an almost helplessly puzzled expression.

Down below, Brand had brought a candle of his own forbidden making and placed it upon an upright barrel to light their discussion. The room slowly arranged itself just as it had been days before, with Duncan and June taking their places near the back so as to better take in the entire proceeding. The same silent stranger was seated in the far corner surrounded by what were obviously his men, the Spokesman at the forefront of them. They looked anxious to begin.

When the room had mostly filled out, Hector rose and stood at the center of them, the candlelight casting dark shadows across the room and making him only one black silhouette among many.

He tapped on the barrel. "Gentlemen, thank you for coming tonight. Last time we gathered I told you Ashmere was a place of many mysteries, Lord Titus's door in the mountain being chief among them, and we together decided to wait for further research from the Circle. But I called you here tonight to announce a new development, for two of our own in this very room took it upon themselves to do some research for themselves, and they believe they are but one step away."

He gestured across to where June and Duncan sat, and the pair related their story from Julian to Mira to the myrtle. She left out only the band of Lord Titus, a dream so vivid she did not remember waking up. Whatever it was that truly led her out to the hidden grove of the myrtle, June knew that relating it to this group would only be to her story's detriment.

Shadows hid many of the faces that appeared to be listening, and June had a hard time reading the crowd before her. However, upon the Spokesman's very shoulders she could see the weight of incredulity, the contrarian waiting to burst forth.

And when she was finished, he did. "So what's our next step, then?"

"If we can bring Mira to the myrtle, then she can lead us to the door."

"If it's so close to the tree that a woman in her nineties could walk to it, why could you not find it when you were at the tree?"

"The eastern forest is thick, sir, and grows only thicker and darker the further into the foothills one goes. And what's more, we gave our word to Mira that if we were to find the tree, then we would bring her to it."

He turned to the rest of the gathering. "Friends, have any of you met the Mira of which they speak?" Here and there heads shook in silent response. "She's an old recluse, older than anyone else in the city. She lives with visions of grandeur of her younger days that I fear may not have happened the way she says."

June could not help herself. "Julian is one of the most respected names in Titus Bay, and he named Mira himself. What she says is true."

"Dear girl, don't you see? Julian's as close to

appointed as the common citizen can be. He's as much a part of the problem as they. The common citizens are being oppressed, and we're wasting our time seeking out Lord Titus, a man dead now sixty years, to save us?"

He gave her no time to respond. "This cannot be our course, friends. We citizens of Ashmere must act, not react. We can send a message and enact change through meaningful protest. We have great plans in place and have already gathered quite a few others to our cause—downtrodden craftsmen like you who gather in dark places to try to remember a better time. But we few can't do it alone. There can't be those who stand neither with the appointed nor with us while they wait for Lord Titus. It takes all of us."

Trying not to make her movement too apparent, she glanced to her side where Duncan stood. Like a scholar considering the philosophies of some lost tome, he took in the Spokesman's words with his eyes closed. While the stranger continued his sermon, June tried to see from her lover's point of view. As neither a craftsman nor guild member, Duncan had very little at stake in the heavy hand of taxation with which the appointed led the city. But he saw the parallel in his own stewardship. Having the library so large a part of his life, Duncan had come to value the knowledge therein. And now older, he was beginning to realize just how much knowledge had been purposely removed. He saw it every day in the empty shelves that he could not fill, the chains that once attached to books that now hung barren. To him it was simply territory lost—and territory lost to the appointed was territory to never be regained.

Hector stepped forward again, his demeanor

passive but imposing. "Dear Spokesman, you miss the point of our gathering tonight, I'm afraid. Your words do sound marvelous, I must admit, and certainly designed to stir our hearts to treasonous action. Just this week we've seen the citizens of Titus Bay worked into a frenzy over the most recent words of the Circle, with *many* traveling beyond the city to search for the door. This isn't inaction, sir Spokesman. You may not think Lord Titus is out there, but many do, and they're not idly waiting for him to save them as you say." He gestured again to June and Duncan. "Our very own have been among those caught up in action, and have found, in my opinion, quite a substantial lead. Would you agree with me, gentlemen?" Hector's voice had by then grown to a reserved shout, as if his own words, said loud enough, might wash away any effect the Spokesman had on the audience.

By June's measure, the loud tone worked. Heads were nodding more vigorously than before, and the flame of the candle jumped with each brief shout of agreement. Had they been in a tavern, June thought, she could imagine them all lifting their glasses to the old librarian. For not necessarily believing in something, the man was almost *too* competent in his ability to convince others.

As the flame spun in the rushing breath of dozens of men, June watched the Spokesman, clearly overruled, return to his seat. He looked behind him to the silent man, whose face showed only a hint of disappointment.

Meanwhile the crowd slowly turned to June and Hector.

One asked, "When will you take Mira out to the

tree?"

"If they're going out to find the door," said another, "I must insist on coming too—if only to see it with my own eyes."

"We might as well all go. This is history in the making."

"Gentlemen," Hector said, "it may be wise for a number of us to stay behind. So large a group leaving the city is sure to draw unwanted attention from the chief constable."

As Hector calmed the crowd, June looked over to see their excitement had somewhat invigorated Duncan. He said nothing, but he stood a little taller, his head held just slightly higher.

For his sake, she knew they could not afford to wait.

12. MIRA AND
THE MYRTLE

As it turned out, there were no volunteers to stay behind while the rest went on to find the door. To avoid the attention a group of citizens might draw the next morning in leaving Titus Bay together, they arranged for June and Duncan to ready Mira while all who wished to accompany them gathered at the cemetery that lay along the northeast highway just beyond the city gates. Rather than pouring through the city gates at once, they hoped a slow trickle might help them go unnoticed.

Unlike their first visit, Mira needed no time to come back to life. She was just as they had left her, burning with the hearth of a much younger woman, and they further stoked the fire with the tale of their discovery. But before they could finish the story she was out of her seat and readying herself for the journey.

Though the morning sun was yet warm, the wind of impending autumn was at it again, so June and Duncan wrapped the old woman in a thick wool shawl they found in a chest that sat in a dark corner of the room. Her steps were steady and she was fast for her age. Nonetheless, Duncan clutched her elbow and helped her down the two steps that separated her door from the ground. As if he knew which horse the old woman would ride, the same curious cat sat upon the horse's hind, observing their approach. His tail still bobbed in an unnerving manner that June could not help but notice.

June had once again borrowed horses from the city stables, this time taking a third along for Mira. A trek out to the foothills was certainly not an errand of the city, but she tried to reason with herself that no one would miss the horses for one day.

Once they had Mira firmly planted in the saddle, they promptly followed the west highway back toward the center of the city. They rode on either side of her, each ready to reach out and catch her should she tip one way or the other. All their talk of Lord Titus might have invigorated the old woman, perhaps even returning a few years into her old bones, but it was impossible to know just how far that new life went. Mira seemed lucid for the most part, but even on their ride across Titus Bay June noticed the old woman fall silent and stare listlessly as her awareness came and went several times.

Once the three passed the city gates and the dense

houses grew sparse, they could see a substantial gathering far off in the distance where the gradual incline toward the forests of the east began. Out ahead of them, planted bestride the highway, was Titus Bay's cemetery.

The group fell in behind the three as they passed by the cemetery, and as June looked back to see who exactly comprised the group, she realized how strange it was to see them so clearly. She had become rather familiar with many of their faces half hidden in shadow. Now fully exposed in the broad light of day, they willingly risked their identities.

But not the Spokesman, nor the silent man to whom he reported. June's glimpse of their faces in the crowd following her was fleeting, and she no more knew them in the light than she did in the dark.

For the sake of Mira's aged body, they rode slower than they might have otherwise. Knowing the old woman to be the key to finding the door at last, the group refrained from complaint, for they had known when they set out that morning that the trek would take most of the day. They kept pace and thinned out as the train of horses carried them further and further toward the mountains.

After a few hours and nearly as many stops to rest for the old glazier, Duncan rode in step with Hector a short way behind Mira and June who headed the procession. Throughout the morning, the old woman had spoken to June very little. When she did it was in streams that started strong but seemed to tire the woman until her silence marked the end of the conversation.

The silent monotony of the midafternoon saw June drifting in one moment and out the other, her hands petting the cat who had since found a place on her saddle.

"Linas likes you," said Mira, her words nearly startling the daydreaming June.

"Oh, his name's Linas? Well yes, he must have taken a liking to me. He's already followed us out here once before."

"I found him in the eastern wood, you know. So, I imagine it's like going home for him."

"You found him?"

"Or he found me, rather. I was out in the forest searching for the door once and I got lost. I wandered for hours before I happened upon him, just sitting there waving his tail the way he does. He led me back to the trail and has stayed with me ever since."

"How long ago was that?"

"Oh, thirty years ago, perhaps. I can still see my hands shaking. They were just beginning to wrinkle." She held her hand, pale and gnarled and covered with creases. "They've come a long way since then."

June smiled and looked forward down the road, trying to get back into her thoughts. Mira's hand then rested upon her shoulder, and the old woman leaned in from her saddle.

"Something's changed with you and the boy."

The statement caught June by surprise, but she did not rush her answer. "I know—I've felt it too. It's this business with the door, I think. It's stirred something in him, some need to be involved in this movement against the appointed." She turned and pointed to the crowd following along the highway. "That's what all this is, you know."

"Oh, of course I realize that, dear. But I'm an old woman and have nothing to lose in such treasonous journeys. Why would a man like that let his son be carried off in such grand ideas that could get him hanged?" She was speaking of Hector.

"That's his uncle—his mentor. From what I've heard, his father too was an outspoken critic of the taxes levied by the appointed. But the summer cough took him—"

"As it's taken so many before their time."

June peered sideways at the old woman. June felt her mind suddenly opening, as if the old woman, with great wisdom and so few words, already knew the root of Duncan's discontent.

"And he died without having changed much of anything; he left no mark to remember him by." She looked back over her shoulder to where Duncan chatted with his uncle. He did not notice her turn around.

"You're looking at the mark he left to remember him by."

"I think you're right, but good luck convincing *him* of that. I just hope that seeing the door might help him find some small measure of contentment."

"For some people—dare I say *most* people—there is no contentment to be found. Life is but a long series of choices, dear, and choosing one opportunity means you lose another."

"You've lived with your own choice all these years."

"There's no way through this life that avoids loss, and there's no way that leads to true contentment. Most of life, every choice you make, will bring some sense of loss. But every once in a great while, if you wait long and make enough choices, life might just present you with an opportunity to gain back some measure of what you've lost."

"And you hope to reunite with the love you lost so long ago."

"I hope to see Titus again, but even if I do, I'll never have back all those years I spent alone."

Out of the corner of her eye June saw the sparkle of a tear running down the old woman's cheek. She let the silence be, trying to imagine what it might be like to be in such a strange love story. Her own story reminded her of Great Gytha's husband, riding headlong toward a cliff in the dead of night. She felt blind to the possible fate that might await her.

A few moments passed and June again broke the silence. "What was he like?"

"Titus? That's quite a question, dear, and not one easily answered. They said he was a ferocious soldier in the great war, and I saw some of that ferocity in his removal of the old king's consuls who watched over Ashmere. But he was also kind and thoughtful, and loyal to no end. It was the type of loyalty that *makes* men ferocious, if you ask me." She paused a moment, and June knew the old woman was imagining the man she had lost so long ago, the man now worshipped by so many who never knew him.

"At times his voice boomed like the cannons of the old world, while at others he was quiet like the flapping of bee's wings. And for all we worked to force him into the mold of a normal man, some wonder followed him that none of us could understand."

"So it's all true then? The things they say about him."

"He wasn't one of us, you know. Back in my youth, before the great war, ships came and went from the bay like the scurrying of mice to a sweet cheese. One of them bore him to Ashmere, and why he came to love us so I'll never know. He never told me of the land of his birth, nor of his parents. I never knew the boy he was, nor why he had stowed away on the ship that brought him here. I only ever knew the man already grown.

"But wherever he came from, and whatever wonder touched him in his youth, he carried it with him to Ashmere. We could scarce understand such things in those days, you see, for Ashmere was never a land of wonder. We didn't know it before him, and I daresay we didn't recognize it until soon after he left. But we all know it now—we all see it so often in our dreams."

It was nearly evening when they passed through the same ruins of the mining town and followed the faint trail through the brush to where the long faded banner hung from the posts, marking the entrance to Lord Titus's amphitheater. As they passed certain landmarks along the way, Mira would interrupt her own remarks to announce her memory of the place, faint though it may have been.

With the ground before the stage sod thick with grass, the entire group dismounted and left their horses to wander the lower levels of the amphitheater. Helping the old woman down to the soft soil below, June and Duncan offered an arm on either side of her, and she took both to steady herself as she walked, half leading and half following June into the darkness of the thick forest beyond the stage.

As they followed the path June had walked in her waking dream, she looked behind and realized she was leading her own parade through the forest. What was quite a long walk the first time was now excruciatingly slow at Mira's aged pace. Careful with her steps, as if she were not holding onto two others, the old woman led with her right foot, bringing her left only so far as to match it and allow her to lead out with the right again.

But when the myrtle finally came into view Mira seemed to shed the ancient gait and strode boldly forward, as if carried by some wonder herself. She put her hand on the massive trunk and walked around it, ducking her silver head under the branches that shot out from its side.

Her hands stroked the rough branches as she passed—not to feel, but to be felt. Her aged eyes inspected the bark, and looking for some mark she must have remembered from all those years before. The crowd moved to encircle the enormous tangle that was the tree as they watched her move with more grace than she had in years, and when she finally found whatever she was looking for she stopped. The branch was low and thick and ran out quite some distance before arching upward to meet the other treetops. She followed the branch outward, keeping a hand on it as one might hold onto the rail of a bridge.

She continued in a straight line well beyond the reach of the branch, lifting her feet as she waded through the thick brush. She reached and touched trees along the way, but only certain older trees, those June suspected the old woman recognized.

"Here you are," they heard Mira say to herself, and all within earshot waded forward to where she stood gazing down. She was kicking away the leaves before her, revealing a white stone path. Its surface, now cracked and splintered like the others in the town down the hill, was embedded into the forest floor, and they followed it further and further as the walls of the foothills narrowed and they found themselves at the bottom of a steeply climbing ravine.

Each step was becoming a struggle, and Mira held tighter to June and Duncan as their march into the heights of the foothills curved ever upward. June knew she was higher than most would ever be and turned to see if she might catch a glance of Titus Bay down below in the distance. And as she looked down upon the straggling followers below, each moving at his own pace, she took in the true size of the mountains. They were but ants climbing up between the sprawling roots of some great tree.

Dusk was approaching, and golden light was soon streaming its way in to light the pale stone path that by that point was mostly whole, only interrupted here and there by the intruding roots of younger trees.

"Almost there," Mira muttered, and no sooner than June heard her than she noticed the walls close in to the width of a single person. Mira stepped through first and June and Duncan followed. It was a hidden glade hidden by rock walls that were covered in vines and overgrowth. Wild grass covered the ground, though only a few trees grew in one patch on the far side, where June supposed the light of the afternoon sun could reach in, if only briefly, each day.

And as June's eyes wandered from the trees to the rock wall that encased the glade, she saw that their trek was over. She let out a sigh and looked over to her Duncan, wide eyed and silent as he followed the old woman across the soft soil of a glade untouched for decades.

They had come to the door.

13. THE DOOR OPENS

June and Duncan were careful not to overtake the old woman as they approached the door, and by the time they reached it much of the group had caught up to them. The gentle glow of the day's close was gone now, and here and there a few men lit lamps to cast some light upon the door. It was a great slab of wood darker than any June had ever seen in Titus Bay, with no decorative lines or adornments. It bore only two distinct features on its surface: an iron handle and a keyhole.

Moments of silence passed as they all considered the sight before them. This was the door of Lord Titus. It was the object of the Circle's research and obsession. It was hope for those who felt themselves oppressed—and a threat to their oppressors. Everything they sought lay through the tunnel just behind the door.

Duncan was first to break the reverence, stepping past the old woman who had stopped to wipe the tears from her eyes. He laid a hand upon the black handle and pulled, and though his body swung backward his hand stayed and he jerked to a stop. He repeated the strangely silent movement again, but to no avail.

"It won't even budge. It must be locked."

"It wasn't enough to hide the door," one rough man said, "but he had to lock it too?"

Another approached. "Move over, boy." He was almost certainly a tree-cutter, June thought, as his wide shoulders hinted that he was more ox than man. He grabbed the handle over Duncan, forcing him out of the way, before repeating his own rendition of the backwards lurch. He did not know he danced, but June thought she could almost hear the music and could not help but laugh.

"Of course it was locked, good sir," said Mira. "Titus always kept his key close so that he could lock the door behind him."

Another voice spoke, and June recognized it as the Spokesman. "Were there other keys? How do we get through?" She looked for him in the crowd, though the lamps in were held so low as to cover many faces in shadow. June could feel a certain wonder in the air, and as she watched the others she saw many heads turning this way and that. They raised their lamps above their faces, searching for the source of the faint music she then realized she was still hearing.

"It's the band of Lord Titus," June announced.

The Spokesman held his own lamp toward her. "How is that possible?"

As it grew louder and louder, many of the men showed their nerves, turning about to face the darkness. Amid the chatter and confusion, June saw Mira move forward and lay a hand upon the door to brace herself. She moved to help the old woman, but when she got close she saw the old hands reach deep beneath the shawl only to reveal a key.

Seeing that only June had seen her, Mira leaned in close. "I only said I'd help you find the door, dear. Each of us has to find our own way through it."

With that she thrust the key into the door, turned it once, and withdrew it. She then pulled the heavy slab open just wide enough to slide her slender body through the gap and into the black—and in the space of two breaths Mira was gone. The sound of clashing metal pierced the door and shook June's insides, and she knew from the sound that the old woman had locked the door from the inside. The music was gone, and everyone turned toward the door.

Where two had just been, there now stood only one.

In a matter of moments, the glade transformed. The glade, which had been silent as the crowd listened to the wondrous music in awe, was now a battlefield as the shaken men rushed the door. They wrenched against the rock face surrounding the door, yet the it did not budge. It did not even make a rattling sound.

As June watched them strain against it, she wondered if perhaps there was some unknown wonder holding it. So tightly shut it was that they might as well have been trying to pull a brick from the walls of the town hall with their bare hands.

She nearly laughed again at the notion, and she knew ultimately that only the key would open the door. No number of clenched teeth, pounding fists, or prying bars could force it open. Some were already beginning to tire, breathing heavy and cradling their bruised hands as they stepped away from the door. She looked away to find the Spokesman standing before her. Her smile quickly vacated, and she looked on the towering man with an overwhelming sense of unease.

"Mira betrays us and you just let her walk right through the door," the Spokesman growled at June. Over the shouting of the crowd and the pounding and prying on the door, she could scarcely grapple with the unexpected attack.

Hector stepped in front of her. "Sir Spokesman, there's no way these two could have known the old woman's true intent." He raised his arms as if to calm the crowd. "Now if we'd just settle down now, we can—"

"I think we've had enough of your leadership," the Spokesman cut him off. "You've sought to keep your hands clean in all this, but you can't. We've all just aided a citizen of Ashmere in breaking our laws of seclusion. We've all committed treason this night, and none of us is safe should we be found out."

As the Spokesman's raised his voice the pounding stopped and the crowd turned their attention from the door to him. "There is a much larger plan afoot," he looked over to the silent man, "and I think we've indulged this door business long enough."

"But the Circle—"

"We *are* the Circle. For months, we've been

masquerading as anonymous scholars, printing our false research in hopes of fomenting resentment for the appointed. We hoped this widespread tension might come to a head and the citizens would demand reform. And it worked beautifully, friends. Citizens have been scouring the hills in hopes of finding a way out of Ashmere for weeks. And every moment they've spent looking for the door is a moment they've spent contemplating the oppression of the appointed.

"That this door actually exists came as a shock to us, for all our *research* was pure fabrication. But if Mira spoke the truth, and there are truly more keys in Ashmere, then let the citizens find them. But until then we can wait no longer. We are proceeding as originally planned, and all are welcome to join who are men of action—not of fables and fancy"

14. A NEW MAYOR
IN TITUS BAY

In the face of sudden and incredible
disappointment, Hector had lost control of the group,
this much was obvious. Where the Spokesman's
words had failed to convince the gathering on June's
first visit to the library cellar, those dark moments in
the secret glade found them all too persuasive, and
many shouted and raised their fists in support of his
radical, if yet still unannounced, plans. June
considered his words as the crowd retraced their steps
down the mountain back to their horses at the
amphitheater. Given his words at the first gathering,
and the number of guildmasters in attendance, June
fully expected many of the guilds to declare a strike

the next morning.

Hector came up behind June and Duncan as they walked and put a hand on each of their shoulders.

"We ought not move any faster or slower than this lot," he spoke in a low, hushed tone for only them to hear, "lest they think we're off to tell the chief constable. I've got a bad feeling about the silent one, as if he may be dangerous. There's something about him that speaks to the extreme, and we may be wise to distance ourselves from this new band of followers he has assembled from our group."

"Whoever he is," June said, "he has no interest in the door unless someone finds the key for him, so we should be safe to move forward with our own search for it. But if you feel he's that dangerous, perhaps we *should* take this to Uncle Ly."

"We must be careful, June. That we were ever associated with this silent man may be unsafe as well. As the Spokesman said, we have aided someone in committing treason. The chief constable has a certain amount of power within his office, but even *he* won't be able to help us if the public thinks us traitors like these. We'll be hanging at the gallows with the rest of them."

"Unless they succeed," Duncan pointed out. "Perhaps the silent man's plans will turn the opinion of the public against the appointed, making us no longer traitors. These laws of seclusion aren't natural. They were instituted for a certain set of people, and if those people change then the law doesn't have the same power. We're only traitors so long as the public thinks these laws mean anything."

"And if we're caught before the tide of opinion has turned? What then, nephew? What his plans are only Titus knows. But he used us to recruit others to his cause, and that very well could hang us. Or me, at least." He swallowed hard after the last word, and June looked up to find the librarian more distressed than she had ever seen him.

Hector stayed near for the rest of the night, never leaving them to converse with any of the strangers that surrounded June and Duncan in the long train back to the city. They said little as they rode through the starless night, but his words echoed in June's head. She thought, perhaps for the first time, of her own death. She wondered how she had missed the gravity of her quest, the treasonous implications and the possible consequences thereof. If they were found out, would the chief constable, her Uncle Ly, truly have no power to save her from the noose? And if he *could*, could the same be said for Duncan and Hector?

This chilled June more than the breeze of the autumn night. She hugged her cloak close, Linas still and content in the warmth of her curled arms. She whispered to the cat all through the night, telling him secrets, her fears and desires, hoping to stave off the worst of thoughts until some unknown predawn hour found her back in her own bed.

The next morning found June tangled in her wool covers, waking to the gentle nudge of her father's hand upon her shoulder.

"June," he said, "get up, girl. The mayor passed away while you were gone last night. They've called the citizens to gather at the square. Hurry and walk with us."

From the look of the light peeking in through the shutters, June knew she had slept well into the day, though she still felt less than rejuvenated. After days of what felt like nonstop motion, she just wanted to rest. And with Cale still out beyond the city, it was the perfect time to make up for lost sleep.

She made no great effort to dress quickly, ambling about to eventually find a dress to slip over her shift. It was a red so pale from age it was easily mistaken for pink. She did not mind the faded color, however, as it was her favorite dress. It was said that in the time before Lord Titus, merchants from foreign places brought their fancy dyes to Ashmere, and in those days, there was no shortage of colorful dress to be seen around the city. But dye-making was not a skill ever learned by the citizens, and soon after Lord Titus closed the bay there was no more dye to be found in the hidden country. Most dress in June's day were shades of brown, as some clothiers had found ways to dye linen with rudimentary tea mixtures. Old garments like June's, plain and faded as they all were after so many years, were prized possessions for families like the Gladwells who did not have many clothes at all.

When she was done admiring herself she went out to the main room where her father and mother stood waiting. As they walked up the path leading to the highway, June caught some movement out of the corner of her eye. It was the familiar sway of Linas's tail above the wild grass. She ran over to where he hid in the grass, likely stalking some field mouse, and picked him up.

She then saw Mira's empty cottage just beyond the trees and she remembered what had happened the night before. Scratching the top of his head, she whispered, "You can stay with me now."

With the cat now quite comfortable in her arms,

June rejoined her parents as they turned onto the highway. Many other citizens had obviously heard the same news and were making their own way to the city center.

"If the mayor died only last night, how did the news reach all of us so quickly?"

"Perhaps they dispatched the messengers to spread the news this morning. Tinkin knocked on our door this morning and told us. It was at what I'd consider a decent hour for a person to be awake." Her father spoke in jest, she knew, but the words came with a small bite.

"I can't imagine another set of parents who has to worry when their daughter doesn't return in the night," her mother said. "What, in the name of Titus, could be keeping you so late?" Her mother was prone to anxiety over such things, and though June was twenty, this did not put the woman at ease.

"The bookkeeper's duties call me beyond Titus Bay, and I can only go as fast as the horse can take me. Believe me, I'd rather be in bed at a decent hour than out riding in the cold."

"You don't think it's dangerous to be out on the highway alone?"

June laughed. "What do you think will happen, mother? That brigands are lying in wait to rob passersby? There hasn't been crime in Ashmere since Lord Titus—"

Her father interrupted, "I wouldn't be so sure, June. Ly came over just yesterday, told me he's in the middle of an investigation right now. Couldn't tell me much about it, but from how many deputies he's charged to help him I'd say there's something going on."

"How many does he have?"

"Fifteen, he said. He's split them into teams, working on tasks all about the city. Whatever's going on, I think even he feels overwhelmed—like he needs all the help he can get."

"Regardless," she said, "my business beyond the city is done for now."

It grew harder and harder to hear one another as they approached the central square. Daytime in the square usually saw a mob of merchant vendors peddling their sundries from carts and stalls. But with the gathering at the steps of the town hall, which stood on the south side, most of the merchants were crowded into the back half of the square, waiting to expand once the mass of citizens vacated.

Perhaps intended to be a grandiose show of power in some forgotten age, the doors to Titus Bay's town hall stood at the top of at least two dozen steps— certainly enough to make visible any speaker who stood at their head. From where she and her parents fell into the crowd, June could see a small group standing somber as they waited to address the citizens. Though she recognized only her Uncle Ly, she knew the rest to be the city councilors who led the city.

Soon a single man stepped forward from among them and lifted his hands to silence the murmuring crowd, and they followed the unspoken request.

"Fellow citizens, we do not wish to speak long today, but we have some very sad news to share. Our beloved mayor, Aster Norfolk, passed away last night. The summer cough, which for months ailed him, has finally taken him, and at the very least I can say I'm glad he suffers no more." June could hear a subtle pain in his voice, the sadness of losing a friend. And though she did not know the councilor, she knew there were plenty of people who knew the mayor and loved him and felt strangled by the loss.

"When Lord Titus appointed the leaders who would carry on in his stead, he made clear that appointed offices should pass from one generation to the next, and that no office should ever be vacant. Since our good mayor was not married and had no children, however, his mantle shall be taken up by his brother."

He took one step to the side. "Fellow citizens, I present to you Mayor Grant Norfolk." A figure stepped forward to stand beside the speaker, and June's heart sank.

Standing poised and bold before the mass of citizens was Ashmere's new leader, whom June recognized from her nights below the library.

It was the silent man.

15. A CALL FOR
THE KEY

"Dear friends," the new mayor began, "I wish it were under better circumstances that I addressed you today. I will miss my brother, and though he is gone I will go about my duties with the same diligence and vigor as befits the office of mayor—just as he did. I want to promise you now that I intend to change our government's burden on the guilds and the common citizens. I know it will be an uphill battle with the council every step of the way, but if you're ever unsure of where you stand on the issue, just remember how dark your homes have been lately thanks to the candle tax.

"But I must say, I know where most of you stand.

I've heard tell of many of you searching for the door in the mountain, chasing that hope that Lord Titus might return to set right what has obviously gone awry in his absence. I have read the findings of the Circle of Scholars concerning the door, just as most of you have, and I believe we are closer than ever to finding the door. But until then I say we enact change for ourselves."

His final words were lost on June, but she heard as the crowd clapped in support but remained collected as a whole. Though his words were well constructed, his delivery lacked any real impact. That he used the Spokesman to persuade tired men in dark cellars to join his cause was suddenly not a mystery. Men of action have no need to be persuasive speakers, and he was just that: a man of action. The sudden death of his brother could only mean one thing.

The good mayor did not die of the summer cough; he was murdered.

After the mayor's words, the citizens dispersed like a deluge, pouring from the square into the connecting streets to go about their business. June found Duncan about his own work in the library and pulled him aside, as if there were patrons who might overhear.

"He's responsible for the mayor's death," she told him.

"June," he said, his voice as calm as the empty library, "nobody killed the mayor. He's been sick for months—you know that."

"He tells us they are setting their plans in motion and the next day the mayor's dead? It's too convenient. There's something sinister going on here, Duncan, and we should do all we can to not be involved."

"It just looks convenient, love. But there's no sinister intent here. The citizens want change, and as the new mayor, Grant Norfolk can help more than ever before."

"They're going to get caught. And when they do, I don't want you to be with them."

"The citizens are speaking with their feet, June. They're lighting their homes with secret candles and meeting below taverns and libraries to discuss notions of freedom."

"I don't know, Dun. I've walked through the city streets in the night, same as you. I didn't see any candlelight through the door cracks."

He went on. "Tomorrow, when the Circle challenges the citizens to find the key, they'll begin to search their cellars and attics. What we've done might be against the law, but it's the law we're protesting in the first place. Seeking to open the door isn't inherently bad. The appointed just stand to lose the most should we actually open it."

"And what if the appointed stop him? You've heard as well as I that the chief constable is conducting some secret investigation. What do you think that's about? He's looking to root out the leader of the rebellion before it gets started."

"Well then we better make sure to not get caught." He paused a moment, and the way he bit his cheek told June he was about to speak candidly. "June, look around you. This library is in shambles because of the appointed, but this is what I stand to inherit. My father died too young—he couldn't pass anything on to me. This is all I have. But it's too late to change what they've done to this place. But if I can keep them from doing likewise to this city that I love, then

I'll help this movement in any way I can."

"I'm just worried about you—"

"I know," he said, taking her hands in his. "But you don't need to worry about me. This may be my only chance to do some good in Ashmere. We just want things to be better for the common citizens, and if we're caught before all is said and through, I can't imagine the masses would hold that against us."

"I hope you're right," she said, throwing her arms around his chest. She knew she could not change his mind, and tears filled her eyes as she left him to his duties in that cold hall. The only consolation she could find was the hope that this secret movement, involving the new mayor and various guildmasters, might have little use for the young librarian. It was the only way he might avoid sharing their fate when June took the matter to her uncle Ly.

She wasted no time in marching herself Uncle Ly's home which lay across the river in the eastern reaches of Titus Bay. Whereas the Gladwells' home was large for the type of cottage that dotted that land in outskirts of the city, the Eastberry family lived further out on what could only be described as a manor. All appointed officers were provided what many of the common citizenry considered lavish living conditions, but when it came to the chief constable she had never noticed. Perhaps it was the recent events that had her mind grappling with aggressive attitudes toward the appointed, but as she approached the house, its enormity struck her as out of place. She shook the feeling before she knocked on the door.

It was his wife, Joyce, who answered. It must have been a day about the house, June thought, for she wore but a grey linen dress almost as plain as June's own. Only on rare and uncertain occasions would such a woman as Joyce Eastberry be seen in anything less than her finest.

"June, dear, how lovely to see you." The woman's smile showed her delight as she discovered June on her doorstep. It was almost too much delight, June thought. She was a sweet woman, no one could deny, and she wanted desperately to be an Aunt to June in the same way Lyman was an uncle.

"Hello, Aunt Joyce. Is Uncle Ly around? I have a somewhat urgent need to speak with him."

"You know, he actually had a visitor this morning and is gone now beyond the city. He said he may be gone a day or two, dear. Is there some message I can give him when he returns?"

"No, that's quite alright. I'll find him once he's back."

After some extended small talk with the woman, June headed back to the Union hall. Since the chief constable was out beyond the city, she would just have to wait to reveal the scandal to him. Until then, she thought she might as well get back to her work. In the same near-constant motion that had deprived her of precious sleep, she had also shirked her duties, and since she could not catch up on one she would surely catch up on the other.

But as she came off the bridge and turned to enter the central square, something caught her eye. It was off in the distance, but pulsed in gentle waves like Linas's tail. But this time it was not the cat's tale that bounced. It was a large paper nailed to a messenger post across the way. June watched it flap in the breeze as two citizens stood before it, their gaze fixed upon its words. June approached, already knowing it to be a work of the Circle of Scholars.

Yet when she joined the others in reading its
words, she found it to be a document quite different
than those that had come before. It no longer focused
on the search for the door in the mountain. In fact, it
freely announced the door's recent discovery,
attributing the success to the Circle's supposed
research.

June clenched her jaw to keep it from twitching as
she read. Her blood was boiling, and she did not
know why. Though the quest had begun out of a
sense of vanity, that oft-hidden side of each citizen
that seeks fame at all costs, she no longer wanted
credit. It was a vile game the mayor was playing,
pitting the citizens against their leaders. June wanted
nothing to do with it.

After the Circle's self-congratulated ramblings,
there was a brief concession of the door's locked
state, the revelation that Lord Titus had locked it,
leaving an unknown number of keys behind when he
left. Admittedly, no amount of research in the
country's hidden tomes would turn up the keys.
Instead, the paper encouraged every citizen to search
their attics, cellars, and hidden places for any
mysterious keys that had no known lock.

June shook her head. She had to admit, it was a
clever way to play it safe and keep all avenues open as
long as possible. The door was no longer their main
concern; the silent man had made that clear. But they
obviously could not abandon the idea completely.
Thus the rebels could continue with their nefarious
plans, allowing the citizens to find the key for them.
And if the citizens ultimately found no key they
would still be occupied in thoughts of leaving

Ashmere.

16. JUNE WITNESSES
AN ARREST

Many citizens noticed the paper nailed into the messenger post, each coming and going while June stood, incredulous. Her gaze remained on the printed words, but her mind was long elsewhere. What the new mayor had planned, she did not know and could not dwell on. But he had won over many on that night in the hidden glade and, as mayor, stood to gain more to his cause with every speech he gave.

June looked around the square. Only a handful of citizens walked where a normal day would have seen hundreds—no doubt the product of more and more guilds joining the candle-makers by declaring strikes of their own. Had June visited the Union that day she knew she would hear the long list of guilds protesting. As bookkeeper, she was familiar with the chain of supply that connected many of the guilds, and she knew that the remaining vendors would soon be starved of supply and forced to join their fellows.

The citizens were stirring, though the door in the mountain was no longer at the center. The secret of the mountain was not the great hulking door—it was the key.

Her thoughts then drifted to Duncan, but were immediately interrupted by a hand reaching up and ripping the paper from its post. June heard the sound of horses and turned to find a group of men approaching, both in the saddle and on foot. Many of them held papers they had obviously torn from other posts about the city. At their head, she recognized Terrel Landish, the whitesmith. She knew him to be another good friend of her Uncle Ly, and one upon whom he most often called to assist him as deputy when his duties took him beyond the city.

They rode past with purpose, as if with a particular destination in mind, and the one who had taken the paper stiffened his pace to catch up. June followed, leaving some distance between her and the deputy's group, though she did not care if she were noticed.

The group never slowed their pace, with a runner here and there breaking from ranks to tear down another paper as they passed. Soon they stopped before the door of Master Wheelright, the printer. An acquaintance of Cale, the printer had hosted the two bookkeepers on previous occasions throughout June's training. Though the decades-long isolation of Ashmere had effectively put an end to the printing of works of the old world, Wheelright had managed to somehow stay in business all those years when so many other printers failed. In his old age, he rarely ran the press, leaving such strenuous tasks to his employees, but instead spent his time reading and choosing those works to be printed and sold.

She knew Duncan admired the man very much, and every time she looked through his windows to the shelves within, chock full of almanacs, permissible histories, and speculative works, she knew why. They were both in the business of preserving knowledge.

But Landish and his fellow deputies were not interested in admiring the printer's work through the window. They dismounted and pushed their way through the door, the lot of them spreading out inside the shop as if the printer were a criminal wont to flee. With all of them inside, June moved in closer, hiding herself to the side of the window.

"Master Wallace Wheelright," Landish's deep voice carried through the glass, "your presence is required at the courthouse. In the chief constable's absence, the magistrate would like to question you."

"About what?"

"About the Circle of Scholars—and who's handling their printing for them."

"I can assure you, sir Landish, that I am not involved in the printing of any illegal material whatsoever. I can show you my books; all my orders have been recorded—"

"Save your breath, printer. This is the magistrate's order, not mine."

Two of Landish's fellow deputies escorted the printer out of his shop, too occupied by their person of interest to notice June's blatant eavesdropping. A few moments after they left, she heard the sound of rustling of papers and the scratching of wooden tables being moved across the floor, the sounds of general rifling.

"Search the place for any connection with the Circle. The chief constable's sure Wheelright's involved."

By that time a small crowd of passers-by had gathered in the street to observe, and June left her spot suspiciously close to the window and joined them. Now quite unable to hear the deputies inside, she turned to the spectators surrounding her. Heads tilted this way and that as they whispered to one another, their eyes were all fixed on the printer's shop and the men standing at the door.

"Papa, why did they take that man away?" It was a child's voice, and June looked behind her to find a girl no older than eight looking up to her father.

"He must be one of the rebels we've been hearing about."

"What's a rebel?"

"People who don't like our leaders."

"Don't they know Lord Titus picked our leaders? I learned that in my lessons."

"It's been a long time since Lord Titus was here, and most of the leaders he chose have long since passed away. Most of our leaders now are their children. The rebels think it's unfair. They don't want the same families to rule Ashmere forever."

"That *does* sound unfair, papa. Are you a rebel too?"

The father chuckled. "No, girl. Ruling is a hard task—one not many are made for. These rebels would soon find the appointed were the better choice all along. No, I think I'll stick to ruling over our house. With your mother gone, I can barely keep track of you. I couldn't possibly look after our city."

The man led his daughter from the crowd, and June kept her eye on them until they rounded a corner. And for some time after they were out of sight, and as the crowd soon dispersed in boredom, their words hung in her mind like freshly cleaned windows. Though her recent experience with the secret gatherings below the library had led her to believe that discontent ran rampant through the streets of Titus Bay, she now realized it not to be so. Most citizens likely thought just as the lonely father did.

This rebellion the citizens seemed to know of was that same discontent. But it was just a rumor to them. Save for the guild strikes, the common citizens were feeling no effects of the rebellion. It was still just whispers in the streets. And until that moment, standing before the printer's workshop, June had been too close to the rebellion to see it for what it was.

Hector had feared his gatherings beneath the library might be mistaken for rebellion, and thus kept them secret to protect himself and his fellows. But the rebellion truly entered when Grant Norfolk and his Spokesman came to the cellar to spout extreme notions. And with Mira's betrayal at the door, he was able to use their frustration to recruit them to his cause.

His rebels were now woven in the very fabric of Ashmere. They were water-carriers, candle-makers, weavers, librarians, guildmasters, and now the new mayor. The leader of the city was also the leader of the rebellion, and the council still had no idea.

The rebellion was happening from within.

June looked again upon the deputies posted at the open doors and those further inside rummaging through stacks and stacks of paper. With Norfolk having sowed discontent at so many levels of society, it was not unlikely that one of the men before her was also a rebel. She would have to save her news for the chief constable himself.

He was the only one she could trust.

17. A CURIOUS PROCESSION

Whether the old printer was involved in the rebellion or not, June could not say. The chief constable, however, had been conducting an investigation, likely for weeks, and the sum of his findings thus far had led him to the printer. His investigation was another fact she had forgotten entirely. Whereas she had been wholly occupied by the search for the door in the mountain, the chief constable had been engaged in his own mystery, and though she already knew the secret behind the puzzle, he could very well be on the verge of solving it himself. He only needed to finish whatever task currently called him away and return to the city to wrap up his investigation.

The sun was below the mountains, and the Titus Bay was turning the dark golden color of late of evening as June made her way through the mostly empty streets. Beside the distant sounds of the bay, the city was quiet as she walked, and in the silence June could not help but ask herself why she was headed to the city center. The day was all but over, and she would not be doing any bookkeeping that evening, she already knew. Too much was happening to simply go hide behind numbers and sums. A massive conspiracy was afoot, and only she knew its true breadth. Such things do not simply work themselves out. And yet June knew she was in no position to pursue a solution. That must be left to the chief constable and the proper authorities.

At that thought, she almost chuckled. The frustration of seeing a problem and being powerless to fix it was the very same sentiment that drove the rebels.

Back in the central square, she went to see Duncan but found the door locked. Though it was normal for the library to close at dusk, it was unusual for him to finish his duties so quickly after locking up. Across the street in the library's east wing she could see the flicker of a small light inside and thought he might be helping his uncle. But when she knocked upon the door of the east wing she found only Hector, he himself still scurrying about in the light of nearly exhausted candle.

"Where did you get the candle?"

"Oh, Brand gave it to me yesterday. He still has quite a supply saved up in his store room. I know this place well enough to clean it with my eyes shut, but the candle makes it seem like I'm not alone in here. I

139

suppose you're on your way home from the Union. Sums *are* awfully hard to do in the dark." He gave her his usual smile, but she found it less infectious than usual. It did not make her want to smile back. It was his eyes that ruined it, she thought, for they gave away the true hopelessness that was weighing him down, dulling his voice.

"I came by to see Duncan, but he's already left. There's something gotten into him. I don't know how to help."

"Yes," he sighed, "everything has sure gotten out of hand rather quickly. I blink twice and everything's changed. I've always rather enjoyed playing host to philosophical discussions in the cellar, you know. I did it not because I sought to overthrow the appointed, but because I believe in the power of true conversation—the power to learn from others, to see things from where they stand. It was a standing meeting for years. And within a week you getting involved the whole thing has collapsed, with some zealot hoping to incite revolution stealing away many of our fellows who were previously content to simply sit and discuss."

His tone hinted at some subdued anger, but with his current state of melancholy she could not be sure.

"Hector, I hope you don't blame me. I had nothing to do with that. I only wanted to find the door in the mount—"

"Since when are you so interested in the door in the mountain?"

"Since Duncan became so fascinated by these extreme notions of revolution. I had hoped finding the door might sway him away, but it hasn't worked out that way at all."

He stared down, past June's feet, nodding as he considered her words. "So the zealot's stolen away Duncan. What else have I missed today?"

She told him of all she had seen that day, from receiving word the mayor had died to the deputies arresting the printer. He was rather emotionless throughout her recounting, save for when she revealed to him the identity of the new mayor.

At this he stepped close, his eyes as wide as the Sylvain. "Have you told the chief constable yet?

"I only learned this morning. I went to his house to tell him, but he's gone beyond the city for a few days."

"That's good fortune, girl. What do you think will happen when the chief constable arrests the man? He'll drag his followers along too—and Duncan with them."

"Then what should I do?"

"Say nothing to the chief constable for now. Give Duncan time to get tired of the cause. This isn't the first threat of uprising in Ashmere, and it certainly won't be any different than the rest. Most fail to gain any real breath amongst the people and die out with but a whimper. Let Duncan's zeal wear off, and once you have the boy safely out, *then* inform the chief constable."

She shook her head. "You don't understand Duncan. He's compelled by some need to make a name for himself. I can't pretend to understand it fully, but I don't think it will simply wear off."

Hector smiled. It was the same wry smile of the cat who knows more than he ever tells.

"My girl, all young men want to make a name for themselves. You should have seen me and Cale when we were his age. We could ride back then, and hunt. We spent entire seasons in the forests, hoping to become famous for finding the great white stag of our day. That need to be remembered never leaves a man fully, but life does have a way of slowly wearing you down until one day you wake up and accept that you were never meant for immortality. You're not the explorer. You're not the conqueror. You're just...ordinary. And that's quite alright."

June had no response. A silence filled the space between them, and she watched a shine from in his eyes as he stared past her, lost in memories she would never know. It was a glimmer of that whimsy which she had watched slowly drain from Duncan.

At last he came to and, blinking until his tears were quelled, said, "It's a hard realization, but an inevitable one. Give him time."

June left him sweeping, the waning candle making his shadow dance across the vaulting walls of the east wing. She knew he was right. To tell Uncle Ly was to put Duncan in danger, and she was hopeful that this fire inside him would burn out with some time. But in her wanderings through the city that day, she began to feel nearly overcome with some great anxiety. It was as if something were happening all around her, always behind her and out of sight. Whereas her story had ended with the door, she could not help but feel that another story was unfolding in the background, and she was helplessly oblivious to it.

June only hoped that Duncan was not involved. But try as she might to believe that he had gone home for the night, she found herself unable to believe it. Thus unable to simply return to her own home and catch up on much needed sleep, she headed to one of their favorite spots where she hoped she might find him.

The bay moved with a slight pulse that only emphasized the stillness of the decaying docks barely standing above. Duncan's figure was nowhere to be seen below, and June felt the fool for having secretly expected to find him there. So rare is it for two people to be on the same page, that such happenings should only be expected in the happiest of story books.

Instead, June moved listlessly down toward the water, trying desperately to turn her thoughts from Duncan. She passed the final row of shops, Great Gytha's among them, following the stone steps one by one. The nightjars called out their presence from the trees, their songs swirling through the white sway of the tide. The combination made the night air seem busy and emotive, but the moonlight streaming through the branches gave away the illusion.

Down below the walkway leveled out and June came upon Titus's Grave. The moon that night hung low behind the great monument, casting the epitaph in shadow. Knowing she had reached the end of her stroll, for the ancient docks were far too dangerous to walk upon, June leaned on the monument. A breeze came from across the bay, and she closed her eyes. She could not see the words, nor the perfectly engraved key that sat below, but as she ran her hands across the polished stone she could almost hear them:

Look forth and behold undying monument
To Titus
The First and Last Lord of Ashmere
Who proved faithful to all trust of his country and his

people
And who saved them from the tyranny of the old world.
To all generations who seek his testament,
Strike forth and find the key to his return.

When the breeze slowed and softened in her ear,
June heard something from up beyond the top of the
stone stairway. It was the sound of movement,
dozens of feet set off by the erratic jangling of metal.
June climbed the stairs, silent as the very grave she
had just leaned upon, curious to see but with the
intent to remain unseen. Near the end of her climb
she lowered her body to a crawl, at the top peeking
her head over first step to see a long line of men
shackled together, moving in begrudging unison
down the empty street. Leading and surrounding
them were strange men wearing long woolen cloaks,
dark hoods hiding their faces.

June had never seen a person in irons before. It
was a thing of the past, tokens of an age when
Ashmere had criminals and the house of corrections
was used. But as the old prison was just across the
street from where June lay on the stairs, she
wondered if this was their destination. To follow
them further would be to risk detection, so June
remained as she was, sprawled flat across the stairs
with only her eyes high enough to watch the curious
procession over the top step.

As June suspected, the group stopped before the
house of corrections and disappeared into the great
building. She strained to hear them, finding herself
wishing again for the stillness of the night which had
been replaced by growing wind. The trees and bushes
waved in unison above her, their branches scraping

like bones in a stew.

When the hooded figures again emerged, they moved back through the street the way they had come, looking markedly more frantic and hurried than before. June wondered what sort of appointment they rushed to at such a late hour and hurried off behind them.

She did not have far to go, for the hooded group soon turned down a side street that skirted the town hall. When she reached the corner she leaned her head slightly and gazed down the alley with one eye. It was empty. She stayed cautious, knowing that at the other end of the tunnel of shadow was the central square, far too wide for them to cross in the time it would take to walk the alley.

But when she exited the alley and walked out into the square, the hooded men had disappeared. Instead, she heard a curiously distinct sound through the wind. It was the furious slapping of wide feet upon the cobble.

"Miss Juniper, is that you?"

18. A MEETING IN
THE DARK

It was Tinkin's voice that rang out through the wind and shadow, a comfort in a night of growing unease. "What are you doing out at this hour?"

"I don't know, truly. I was just taking a late evening stroll when this storm blew in. Why are you still in uniform? Do they have you working this late?"

"Just a special task from Mayor Norfolk. He asked me to fetch the council and magistrates for a discreet night meeting. Don't tell him I told you." In the shadows June could not see his face, but she could almost hear his winking. "I've summoned the last and am just headed home now."

June let the gangly man continue on his way and promised to return home before she caught a cough.

He was a lovely man, and one with whom June had always enjoyed occasional conversation, but in that moment she would have said anything to see him gone. Between the group of hooded men and the secret city council meeting, there was too much happening to simply stand aside and feign disinterest. And seeing that the place where the former disappeared was the same place the latter was supposed to meet, she knew she needed to be inside.

The wind ripped through the square, whistling as it skidded through the alleys and narrow streets. June could hear the great doors of the town hall heaving with every gust. She crept upward, and from the top of the steps she looked out upon the moonlit square. Save for the leaves dancing across the square, it was still and devoid of life. She would not hear anyone walking for the howl of the air, so she took a moment to survey the moonlit square from her cover of dark.

Clutching her cloak about her, June then turned to the doors. The wind was strong, but not enough to open such massive doors. While one was fastened in place, typically for the other to latch to, the other swung ever so slightly, though never enough for a person to slip through, occasionally crashing into the stone stopper that kept both doors from opening inward. The door was so heavy that its collision with the stopper echoed inside.

She gripped the handle without trying to hold the door, allowing it to continue moving in the wind, and when she felt it about to hit the stopper pushed as hard as she could to make the booming crash even louder. She continued this a few more times, hoping any occupants inside the chamber beyond the entrance corridor might take the repetition as natural.

And when she was confident that they would have ceased to notice the more intense sound, she pulled hard to open the door wide and slipped through.

The door crashed with the same effect as though she had slammed it, and under cover of the booming noise she dashed into the shadows of the corridor. Protected from the gathering storm outside, the jarring of the door was the only sound to be heard. She crossed the dark corridor to the entrance of the chamber and, through the cracks of the old wooden door, saw fingers of light reaching through. Putting an eye to one, she could see two standing torches at the center of the room, giving only the dimmest of light that was so weak that the corners and walls of the great chamber remained in total darkness.

Knowing the councilors would arrive soon, she went further down the corridor and crouched in the darkness. She had heard of emergency council meetings held at odd times, but some of the councilors were the elderly and not in good health. Such a storm would present danger well beyond the ride there and back.

By then the rain was beating down upon the city, and June watched as the door opened and the first weary traveler appeared. With only the light sneaking in through the wavering door, she could not see who it was that crossed the corridor to enter the chamber. She could only count. With twelve comprising the city council and three magistrates in the courts, she knew she was safe from discovery upon the fifteenth entrance.

Once she was sure no others would be following, June crept through the darkness back to the front doors and, pulling the loose one shut, quickly turned a handle to keep it latched in place. Now afforded complete silence from the chaos outside, she returned to the crack in the chamber door.

They were all seated facing the new Mayor Norfolk, who stood above them, the torches lighting just above each shoulder. The light upon his shoulders and hood rendered his face too dark to see.

"What's the meaning of this, Norfolk? Why have you called us here at this hour?"

"Councilors and magistrates," he began, the standard address at formal meetings, "you are here tonight to tender your resignation. As of this night there will be no more appointed, and Ashmere will no longer be subject to the whims of a gluttonous few."

"You have no authority," a hoarse voice rose above the mayor. One of the councilors then stood, tall and broad, as if to charge the mayor. But the mayor snapped his finger, and the hooded men emerged from the darkness to surround the councilors.

"Sit down, Coogan, you fool. I'm not making a suggestion or even giving an order. I'm simply explaining what has happened, the same explanation I will present to the citizens tomorrow. I came into office to be horrified by the council's plans for future taxes and oppression of the common citizen. With such greed and corruption abounding within the leadership, I had no choice but to declare you all unfit for your offices."

"It won't work, Norfolk. This is the system put in place by Lord Titus. He appointed his leaders for a reason. Leaders must make difficult decisions, and difficult decisions are never supported by all—the citizens know that. It can't just be swept away by the likes of you."

"You overestimate their loyalty to you, I'm afraid, and their loyalty to Lord Titus. An iron can only be boiled and cooled so many times before it eventually cracks. Just look around you. Where are the candles that usually light this chamber after nightfall? Where are the vendors in the square? This strike speaks to a less understanding citizenry than, I think, any of you realize. Tomorrow I shall tell them you left the city, and they will clap their hands to see you gone."

"The chief constable—"

Norfolk interrupted, "The chief constable has gone beyond the city on business. By the time he returns it'll be too late. Power will have shifted, the citizens will have accepted your corruption, and *my* men will be arresting *him*."

"Speaking of which—my men here will be overseeing your departure. You are all to leave the city tonight. Return to your estates, take what you can carry and go. We've had sixty years without violence in this city, a tradition I'd like to continue—but please do not mistake me." He nodded to the hooded figures encircling the terrified council. "These men are not afraid to do things most of us shudder to think of for the sake of Ashmere. If any of you are still within the city come dawn, they will make sure you disappear. Either way, there will soon be no more appointed in Titus Bay."

The council was still, the mayor's final words crashing into them as the thunder that shook the very chamber in which they sat. Nobody said a word. The threat was clear. They only sat there in silence, no doubt contemplating their options, though June herself could see none.

It had happened sooner than she expected. It was still his first day, after all. But the mayor was clever. Seeing the chief constable gone beyond the city, he knew this would be the most opportune time to strike. The chief constable was the right arm of the council. He was their instrument. They made decisions and he enforced those actions accordingly. But with the mayor having gathered his own small force of rebels, he surely had the power to run the appointed, deprived of their means with which to defend themselves, out of the city.

She wondered how far the mayor's plans extended beyond the council. Did he plan to drive the rest out after the council? After all, the genealogies of Duncan's library showed that he was one of them. Would she lose him too? There was very little unclaimed land in the hidden country, but in that moment she could almost picture the two of them watching a sunset from their home high in the foothills. It was a lovely thought, though fleeting in the face of the horror implied in such exile.

Then she thought again of her Uncle Ly. He would not go down without a fight, and the night was still young. With the right horse from the stables she could ride hard enough to find him. There was still time. She rose and started for the door when she was stopped in her tracks.

From within the door she heard a familiar voice. "Is that it, then?"

It was the unmistakable voice of Lyman Eastberry.

19. JUNE STEALS THE BAKER'S BEAST

She knelt back down to stick her eye to the cracked door. One of the men behind the mayor pulled back his hood, revealing the lean face of the chief constable. His mustache, black as coal in the waning light and wispy as ever, curled upward with his smile. One by one the rest of the hoods fell. June did not recognize them all, but Norfolk's expression made clear these were not the faces he expected to see.

Norfolk took a step forward through the middle of them as if to bolt for the door, but the chief constable's hand caught him square upon the shoulder and stopped his fleeing feet.

"I'm afraid the game is up, dear mayor. It would be quite useless to run now. But if you'd like to leave, My men here will escort you to a cell in the house of corrections. I've saved it just for you." He gestured to his men, and two stepped forward to take the mayor by the arms. Seeing the mayor now panicked and pathetic caused some unknown joy inside June, and she could not help but burst through the door as the men approached.

As she passed him she could see clearly the shock that had overcome him, and his eyes only rested on her face for but a moment. He had just been caught in a plot against the most powerful people in Ashmere; he knew what fate awaited him.

By the time she reached the center of the room where her Uncle Ly stood, the council and his men had surrounded him. They patted one another and shook hands and congratulated themselves. The chief constable assured them that there was no lingering danger for them. He recommended they gather the next morning when properly rested and discuss a trial.

They were not done with him, but June pushed her way through and wrapped her arms around her uncle anyway.

"Juniper? What in the name of Titus are you doing here?"

"I knew of his plot this whole day. I wanted to tell you, but you were gone. I didn't know what to do. How did you know, uncle?"

"My dear girl, we've been a step behind them ever since they were gathering in a dark little tavern in the northern reaches of the city. Over the months he's cast a wide net and sowed the seeds of rebellion. Once the old mayor passed we thought it the best time to take them. We arrested his printer earlier today, something I had hoped might force his hand in light of my absence. We guessed right."

"So Landish was right to arrest the printer, then?"

"Of course. I had to remain unseen all day, so I couldn't have done it. Terrel's been invaluable in leading the other team of deputies through all this. But that reminds me," he paused a moment and looked into her eyes. He wanted her to hear more than just the words coming from his lips. "This has been a many—faceted rebellion, and though we've succeeded in heading it off on this front, Landish is heading it off on another. I'm not going to ask how you know anything about this or how involved you've been. I *will* say that if anyone you know or care about is wrapped up in all this, you need to go convince them to stay home tonight. With a rebellion of this size I'll have no power to release anyone who's arrested. Their fate will be decided by the court."

"What happens tonight?"

"A trap has been laid—whispers of a key to the door in the mountain. It's a farce, designed by us to draw those traitors to the door. Terrel and his deputies lie in wait for them there."

June did not need to hear more. She rushed through the dark aisle back through the doors and into the rain. Pulling her own hood over her head, she took the steps two by two and crossed the empty square. The few stalls left in their usual places like vendors were collapsed, their leather canopies flailing about like a hound at the end of its leash. The pounding rain moved in wide sheets, combing the mud and filth out of the cobble and washing it ever closer to the river.

She skirted each building as she made her way through the empty city streets to Duncan's home. As she approached she thought she might see a faint light through the shutters, but remembered then the strike that deprived so many of light within their own homes. Looking around her on such a dark night, she still saw no light sneaking out through any shutters.

She rapped hard on the door and was met by Duncan's mother, a nice woman but one plagued by poor health and left the house as little as possible.

"June," the woman shouted over the rain. She grabbed the soaking cloak about June's shoulders and pulled her inside. "What are you doing out in the storm?"

"I need to see Duncan—it's urgent."

"He's not here, dear. I would have thought you had known. He left earlier this evening to go beyond the city." She clutched her forehead as if in pain. "I-I can't remember why. Business, I think. Said he wouldn't be back until tomorrow."

Though she had known the woman for years, June always lamented having never met the true Rosey Westock. Duncan supposed that her heart and mind were broken on the day his father died. The feeble and forgetful woman before her was the only June had ever known.

Duncan sought no delusions in his mother, seeing her for what had become after the cough took his father. She had been an extraordinary woman, he told her, and one happily engaged with the affairs of the city—just as his father had been. He remembered no shortage of love between the two and that the story of their courtship was one for the ages, though he only remembered hearing hints of it in his childhood.

Now, with his father gone and his mother in her condition, the story would be forever lost.

June hurried her exit, assuring the dazed woman that the storm beating down upon her roof, the rage she had seen through the open door, was not nearly as bad as it seemed and that a brisk walk would take her home in a matter of minutes. Back on the street, June held her cloak tight and sprinted to the stables. With the greatest of urgency in mind, and knowing the peril of the storm, she did not even glance at the far end of the dark aisle where stood the horses owned and used by the city.

Looking to the baker's great beast, used to bearing quite a portly fellow, June thought of her own frame. More slight than the baker to say the least, she hoped it might afford the beast some extra strength, thereby cutting the journey in half. But truly she hoped to not have to ride all the way to the door. If Lord Titus had any measure of mercy, she would reach Duncan long before he walked into Landish's snare.

She saddled the beast up and was on her way, finding the rain to indeed be waning, just as she had told Rosey. It gave June an odd comfort to know that not everything she had told the woman was untruthful. As broken as the woman might have been, June always felt deep guilt in telling her what she wanted to hear. It would be one thing if every half-truth were told to bring comfort, but that was not always the case. Sometimes it was simply to avoid answering question after question. It was worthy of the guilt, June knew. Like everyone else, she would rather dismiss the half-mad woman than engage her.

The storm soon abated, though not entirely. With no other sounds but the rain and the quiet clomping of hooves upon the damp earth, June's mind was free to wander as it so often did on those long walks through the city. She thought of Titus's Grave, that grand view she and Duncan loved to enjoy together, before drifting to Great Gytha, the old woman she had only recently met, but wished she had known her whole life.

Though Gytha was nearly thirty years Rosey's senior, they had much in common. They had both been skilled and empowered women in their days. They both been engaged in their communities. They had both lost husbands.

But it was in this loss that they also differed greatly. Being such strong women, they both presumably were more than able to take over in their husbands' absence. But where Gytha had stepped up, Rosey had fallen apart. Was the strength of each of them truly so different?

The more June thought about it, the more it puzzled her. It was hard for her to imagine, of course, as she had never felt such great loss herself. She could only ponder what kind of woman she would be if she were to lose Duncan. Would she find the strength to carry on, or would she be left crippled with nothing to live for?

She hoped to never find out.

20. A RACE TO
SAVE DUNCAN

The night's journey was progressing much faster than their first foray into the forests of the eastern foothills. With exception to the mining camps, the foothills were generally untouched by the citizens, but even in the dead of night June could now see where so much recent traffic had widened and pronounced the once lost paths that diverged from the highway.

Though the night had been no less dark on her first journey to find the door with Duncan, the once unknown paths leading into the foothills were now somewhat familiar. She recognized landmarks as she passed them and, remembering how long the first treks took, knew she was making incredible time. The baker's horse was living up to its reputation.

But June found little comfort in the horse's hastened pace. Every step forward without coming upon Duncan was, for him, another step closer to the deputies' trap. She had to go faster if she were ever going to catch him, but she could not push the horse too far. Much of the remaining journey led uphill. If she were not careful she might exhaust the beast completely.

The logic of her thoughts kept her calm all the way up to the remains of the old mining town, a landmark she still thought far ahead of her. It was just past midnight, by her estimation, and by then the rain had cleared, leaving only a steady wind to barrel through the trees and beat upon the mountains. The moon was just coming over the peaks, and in the illumination June saw horses scattered throughout the old campsite.

Her heart nearly skipped a beat. Knowing themselves to be somewhat close to their destination, Duncan's party must have decided to proceed on foot due to the steepness leading up to the door.

To keep from being discovered lest the worst happen, June took the baker's beast well past the overgrown brush that surrounded the littered meadow. Like those she hoped to catch up with, she proceeded on foot. Lifting the sides of her dress above the forest grass to keep from tripping, June followed the path into the dappled moonlight as silent as possible.

It was all just as she remembered it. The ground leveled out as she followed the rounding path into the amphitheater, and she ran downhill behind the stage, just where she had seen the Vision of Titus. Racing downward, she almost thought she saw a glow of the grand parade again, but as she reached the great myrtle she saw that it was the stone path Mira had uncovered. The flat stones now glowed like the stars, no doubt some revenant of the wonder that left with Lord Titus, and June followed them upward as the mountain walls narrowed into the steep ravine. She could see the softly glowing path lead ever upward until her eyes could not see the darkness separating them in the distance.

It was as June gazed upward that she saw something darken the path well above her, and she knew it was the many bodies of Duncan's party moving along the glowing stone. Her heart sank to see them so much higher than she, for she knew it was impossible to reach them before they came to the door, and with the wind still howling as it was, a shout would not go far.

And so she put her feet upon the glowing stone and raced upward. As she climbed above the trees she did not stop to look back and admire the city in the distance. She did not stop to look out over the land that hid their bay for a glimpse of the southern sea. She did not look up to see that she was failing to close the gap. She only kept her eyes upon her next step.

It was hopeless, she already knew. But if hope is something so easily lost, then what good is it?

June could just see the top of the sheer walls holding the secret glade when her knees buckled and she collapsed upon the stone. Heaving as she caught her breath, she lay her head uphill and kept an eye on the glade walls. They lit up sharply as if one torch had been followed by many, and the wavering light upon the walls looked almost like a brawl.

After only a moment she got back to her feet and proceeded uphill again, but now staying behind the trees that dotted the grassy ravine floor as she went. At the top, she hid herself in the darkness just outside the glade and looked into the glade that seemed carved out of the very mountain. She could see a group kneeling in the center, surrounded by two dozen men holding the torches—the chief constable's deputies.

Standing before the men on their knees was Landish, tall and broad and casting their submission upon the stone wall. He held an open book across one arm, the other scratching something upon its pages.

"It's a long journey back to town. Should any of you somehow escape along the way, I want you to know that we've recorded your names and will find you. Your rebellion is over, I'm afraid. We know about the mayor. We know about the Circle of Scholars. We know who has been involved. And while you spent your night riding out here, Chief Constable Eastberry captured them all. So, come along peacefully, gents. You've lost."

"Please, sir," it was Duncan's voice. "We've come all this way to see the door opened. Won't you at least try it?" June peeked an eye around the tree she hid behind to see Duncan's hand outstretched, holding a key up for Landish to take.

"The key was a farce, you fool." He took the key from the boy's hand and threw it into the darkness. It landed with a thud just behind June. "It was planted to draw you out here. But even if it weren't, do you think I'd take part in your treason? I'd be bound for the gallows like the rest of you." He spit on the ground in disgust, looking sharply at Duncan. She could not see his face, but could only tell that he was meeting the deputy's gaze.

In an instant Duncan was on his feet, sinking his knuckles into Landish's jaw. The larger man reeled backward, from either impact or shock, or both. Before June knew what was happening, the rest of them had joined Duncan, pushing back the deputies surrounding them. In the chaos, June stepped forward, looking for an opportunity to reach Duncan and escape with him. But there were too many men, too many swinging fists.

By then Duncan had grabbed a torch from one of the downed deputies and laid it against the door. The flames washed upward over the hardened wood of the door as Duncan left it to help his fellows. They were hopelessly outnumbered, and when the deputies were no longer taken by surprise, they began to hold their ground, again forcing some of the men into submission, albeit this time with many blows.

As it became obvious the tide was again turning, Duncan's eyes scanned the narrow exit and, for one instant that felt like a hundred, June knew he looked into her eyes. He stood there, a small shadow before the burning door behind him, smiling at his love for perhaps the last time. He did not see her smile back, though, for Landish was back on his feet by then and on the boy, who was clearly no match. Withone strike he had Duncan on the ground and he held him there with a foot upon his chest.

Behind the shouting and fighting of the men, the fire of the torch had grown to completely engulf the door. It now raged with a fury of its own, casting so much light up upon the mountain that were anyone in Titus Bay awake at such an hour they would surely have seen it.

Then came a sharp and heavy clank of metal, a sound June recognized from Mira's betrayal. As the wood was consumed at the edges, the weight of the great door bore down upon the iron latch keeping it shut. The weakened wood gave way, and the latch broke through, causing the burning slab to swing open wide to shocking revelation.

As a teary-eyed June shrunk back into the shadows of the night, the rebels and deputies alike stood together in silent awe, unable to fully grasp the sight before them.

There was no tunnel behind the door. There was no pathway through the mountain. Where the door had once stood, wondrous and immovable, there was only a face of sheer rock.

21. TO LEAVE
A LEGACY

June awoke to the sight of the city already warming itself in the morning sun. She had slept much of the journey atop the baker's beast, who now strode down the northeast highway with a much more relaxed gait. It was as if the horse knew there was no longer any urgency in their travel. They neither pursued nor were being pursued. The beast took its time while its soft cargo drifted between sleeping and weeping.

Tears had not left her eyes since they looked upon the door in the mountain as it swung open in a fury of flame. In her blindness, she turned to tread back down the darkness of the steep ravine. The last thing she heard was Landish screaming at the subdued rebels, "You fools! You plotted, conspired, and murdered—and all in the name of a farce."

His words stayed with her as she hid with the baker's beast in the brush until the deputies and their prisoners had passed. It could not have been a farce, she told herself, for she herself had seen Mira go through the door. She had seen the darkness into which the old woman had disappeared, heard the lock turn from within.

Because Lord Titus so famously used the door, she was not surprised that it possessed some measure of wonder. But how could it open to a tunnel for one and to a stone wall for another?

Perhaps the wonder was not in the door at all, but in Lord Titus. Mira was able to open it because she held his heart, as he held hers. And now she and her lover, the first lord of Ashmere, were reunited. They were together as June and Duncan would never again be.

It was midmorning as June entered the city. Duncan had likely been sitting in a cell within the house of corrections since before dawn. She wiped what tears still remained as she passed other citizens going about their business, reminding herself that no matter how rough her night had been, Duncan's had been worse.

Back at the stables she returned the baker's beast back to its place at the end of the row.

"Thank you," she told the horse, running her hand down its neck, "they were just too far ahead of us."

June had no concern for her work that morning. She only wished to go home and rest. After a week of near constant motion she just wanted to stop.

The square was alight with the spark of recent intrigue, but June took heed of the change as she crossed. She took no notice at all until passing a small crowd gathered about a messenger post. They were reading about the incidents of the previous night, the plot to murder the city council, the chief arrest of the mayor and his men, as well as the burning of the door in the mountain. The council had already met that morning and announced the trial to be in three days. The accused would remain in the house of corrections, with the guards there ordered to turn away any visitors. Evidently the appointed still allowed at least one printer in Titus Bay to print their news. She turned and resumed her groggy path home with scarce a raised eyebrow.

When she came to her home she was met by sideways looks from both her parents.

Her mother clutched her shoulders, looking her up and down. "Were you out all night again? My word, I thought you had simply risen before us to be about your duties this morning."

"Yes," June said, somehow able to hold the tears at bay for her parents. "My work beyond the city took longer than expected."

Her father then asked, "Have you heard what happened?"

"I-I saw it posted."

"Duncan was among those arrested. Did you know he had fallen in with any rebellion?"

"I have," her lips paused as she searched for the right word, "suspected."

"June, I'm so sorry," her mother said. "I know what he means to you."

The tears came again as June moved into the arms

of her mother. "Hector was going to retire soon, and Duncan was going to take over the library. We were going to marry."

"This might just be a blessing," her father said. "I know it hurts now, but it's better for this to happen now than in ten years when the deputies are dragging him away in front of your children. I say good riddance, Juniper. I shudder to think of you with such a man. You're too good for him."

By then she was weeping so fiercely that her agitation at his words were well covered. She knew, after all, that he was only trying to comfort her. He was just ill equipped for such situations, and he did not have the right words. June wondered if anyone had the right words. But no matter his intention, she could not let anyone think that of her Duncan.

"You've known Duncan as long as I, Papa. He's a good man with a heart that feels for everyone what they don't think they're allowed to feel themselves. He loves everyone. He only wanted what was best for Ashmere. He just wanted to be remembered."

At what June suspected was some unseen gesture from her mother, her father was silent. She stayed in the hold of her mother's arms a few moments more before turning in. Something in her own words bothered her, and she reflected on them as she slowly drifted from day into dream.

She thought of Lord Titus, whose legacy had been built up in the decades following his good deeds. Though the legends had grown to treat him as something more than a man, a fact to which even Mira had attested, had he actually passed away as normal men do he might have never known the extent to which Ashmere would base its traditions on him. He had not sought for fame and glory. His legacy had come not by intent, but as consequence.

And as the image of this great man towered over that of her Duncan, June could not help but wonder if he had, in fact, been misguided not only in deed, but in his intent. People are remembered for their selfless deeds. But to be remembered is not a deed in itself.

And as her drifting mind thought about what Duncan wanted, she wondered whether his desires were selfless at all. Perhaps it was not for her to judge another's desires, and she dared not declare her love selfish in a quest for himself. But as coherence slipped from her thoughts, she had one prevailing thought remain as the oddities began to take over:

There are more noble causes than to leave a legacy.

22. GREAT GYTHA

Over the next three days June moved from the
warmth of her bed very little. Linas even joined her at
some point, his tail abandoning its watchtower post as
he curled up against her. At her mother's gentle
insistence, June rose in the mornings and evenings to
take a walk. Every time she set out, aimless and
wandering through the city, she found herself at
Titus's Grave.

It was on these walks through the bustling streets
that June began to hear stories of the rebellion
develop. Rumors ran riot like children skipping home
after their lessons, and with no citizens permitted to
communicate with the accused while they waited trial,
conjecture was fast becoming fact. As most citizens

were completely unaware of the rebellion happening right under their noses, all whispers she heard were but wild speculation—distorted takes on the events June had watched from the periphery.

These rumors grew even wilder, of course, when Hector was arrested on the second day for his involvement. It was only a matter of time, June thought, and he must have known it was coming. Whether he was innocent of intent or not, the chief constable only knew he had played host to Norfolk and his rebels. June could only surmise it was one of them who had divulged his involvement.

She did not witness Hector's arrest; merely hearing of it was too much for her. A person is only given to love so many in a lifetime, and June was fast losing the people she cherished most. Perhaps that was the difference between June and the rest of the citizens, the reasons she wanted to lie down and die while it appeared that everyone else was content to carry on like usual. Whereas they loved first the society Lord Titus had rebuilt for them, she loved first the people—and were she forced to give up one to preserve the other, June would upend society in a heartbeat.

For in the end society is not an entity capable of love or being loved. It is just an agreement forced upon everyone born into it. It is the people that are worth loving, for society is only as strong and good as they, and without them it is but a hollow structure devoid of any true meaning.

It was this meaning that drove her steps on the morning of the third day, mere hours before the trial was set to commence. Just as the other mornings, she sat before Titus's Grave watching the eastern peaks for the sun to rise, desperately searching herself for some measure of comfort. The outcome of the trial was all but determined already. With the council themselves witness to its foiling, the trial was but an adherence to Ashmere's laws, a formality extended for the sake of Lord Titus.

As the sun finally reached its way over the eastern peaks, spreading itself upon the waters, June heard creaking wood behind her. Up the hill, Great Gytha was descending the stairs from her loft to unlock the shop below. Few shopkeepers in Titus Bay lived above their own shops anymore, leaving most lofts in the city to sit empty or be occupied by guild apprentices. With so little crime since the time of Lord Titus, there was no need for shopkeepers to watch for thieves in the nights. Only a few, such as Great Gytha, who remembered the crime of the old world, still lived above their shops.

Climbing the steps up to the shop, June found the shutters and door already open and could see the old woman straightening things up inside as she prepared for the day. She stepped into the open doorway and saw Gytha sweeping, not yet noticing her. The shelves were noticeably more full than before and the entire shop seemed more balanced out by the new wares filling in the gaps.

"I see you're selling candles again." Her voice trembled; she had spoken only a scarce few words in the days since Duncan's arrest. "I suppose the strike was resolved, then?"

Unstartled, the old woman turned to face June, her hands pulling the broom back and forth while her eyes focused elsewhere. "Resolved? No. But it's ended all the same. After they arrested the rebels, the city council wasted no time in letting every guild and merchant know that all movement of goods throughout the country was to begin again at once. *Any who refuse will be brought to trial as part of the rebellion,* they told us. *Commerce shall commence.*"

Sweeping her way to June at the doorway, she turned the broom over and began to pick at the straw. Though she had met Great Gytha only days ago, she felt like an aunt she had not visited in years.

"You know," the old woman started, "I don't get many visitors so early in the morning. What brings you my way, child?"

"I want to know how you do it," June responded. Whereas she had thought herself all out of tears from her crying, she now found more beginning to swell. She fought hard to keep them back. "How do you lose so many people you love and still find the courage to go on?"

"Oh, there's no courage, child. Brave or not, you have no choice but to move on—the rest of the world certainly isn't going to wait. If the world is going to move on, then so must you if you want to remain a part of it. But that was perhaps always my problem—guilt. For to move on with the world means leaving those you lost behind, and it's easy to let such thoughts turn into guilt. It may not show its face for years, but it's guilt that cripples and leaves you broken."

"I've never hurt like this before. I feel as if I'm losing some part of myself."

"And you will, child. You'll feel a great many things before you're through, most of which you'll never be able to explain. There's no easy answer here, I'm sorry to say. Loss is a part of life, as sure as the

172

setting sun, and the darkness that comes after is very real. It takes years to pass for some, decades for others. But it passes all the same."

Just as her mother, the old woman took June into her arms and held her while she wept. Great Gytha apologized for not having the answer, but June thanked her for her honesty above all.

Back outside, June could see the sun fully above the eastern peaks, and headed for the city center. The trial would be starting soon. Under normal circumstances, one of the three magistrates would oversee the trial, depending on which region of Ashmere it had taken place. This, however, was no normal circumstance. Something about this case, some procedure of court June did not know, must have dictated that the council themselves oversee the proceedings.

Thus, June found herself sitting on the town hall stairs awaiting any sign of life from the proceedings within. The late autumn air, though not pushed through shivering bodies by the wind, still held a slight chill, but as June looked around at the others who crowded around the entrance to the hall, friends and families of the accused, she saw none of them were bundled up for warmth. Even the cold of impending winter was no match for the frigid solemnity of losing the ones you love.

After an excruciating hour had passed, one of the great doors of the hall was pushed ajar. The chief constable slipped through the dark opening and took a seat next to June.

"I'm sorry I haven't come talk to you in the last three days. I meant to. I've just had my hands full preparing for the trial."

"Is it over, then?"

"Almost. They're hearing the final testimonies now."

"What's it look like?"

"Not good, June. They're going to make an example of this rebellion."

"What's that mean for Duncan?"

"I plead with the council for him, June. I want you to know that. But it's out of my hands. They refused to spare him the gallows. Tomorrow morning." His hand slid out upon the stone, low so those standing below would not see. Under his palm he revealed a long key. "Take this. It's the chief constable's key to the house of corrections. Go see him tonight after nightfall and say your goodbyes."

"What about the guards?"

"There are no guards. When was the last time anyone was arrested? Until now, the house of commons has sat empty for years. We can't pay guards to watch criminals we don't have. I'll make sure Duncan is placed near the entrance so you're not seen by the others. I must be getting back now."

She slid her own hand out to take the key, concealing it within her cloak, and with a regretful nod the chief constable rose to his feet and returned to the darkness within the hall.

Soon the doors opened and June joined the citizens at the foot of the steps as the accused were led out in irons for all to see. On behalf of the council, the chief constable stood before them and announced the verdict: guilty. His voice trembled, and he spoke not with pride nor triumph as some might have expected. Nonetheless, the crowd around June erupted in almost uniform praise, as any sympathizers were wise not to express their displeasure too loudly.

Amidst the clapping and cheering, June made no sounds. She only looked up to Duncan, the last in the convicted line. He was searching the crowd, likely for her. She hoped to meet his eyes, but by the time the shackled prisoners were led off stage, his had not found hers. Beneath her cloak, June's fingers wrapped so tightly around the key that she could feel her heart beating in her hand.

She would not resign herself to losing Duncan just yet. Her story was not over.

23. THE LOVERS ESCAPE

June passed the rest of the day sitting in silence, her eyes closed as she leaned against Titus's Grave listening to the ringing sound of her fingers tapping the stone engraving. She debated whether she should go through with her plan and speculated at the consequences sure to ensue. The first of her worry was Uncle Ly. That key was entrusted to him as part of his appointed duties, and he had done her a kindness by letting her take it to see Duncan one last time. If her plan did not work, would she ever be able to look him in the eye again? And what kind of punishment might he face once his part in the betrayal came to light?

This was assuming, of course, that the key opened

not only the entry to the house of commons, but the cells themselves. June could very well find the key more limited in its utility than she expected.

But if her plan *did* work, then she would not have to face Uncle Ly again. In fact, she would likely never see him again, nor anyone else for that matter. Her thoughts drifted to an escape from Titus Bay, which was easy enough to imagine. But what then?

She wondered if there were room enough in Ashmere for two young lovers to run off together and remain unfound. And with the tree-cutters harvesting the old forests and planting their own, even the depths of the wood were not safe from accidental discovery.

Her thoughts constantly shifted upon these points as she lay back against the monument, occasionally drifting in and out of sleep. She kept her place there, out of sight of any passersby above, until well after sundown, when the moon was high in the night sky and the streets were lifeless but illuminated.

Once she decided it was the proper time to move, she climbed the steps and crossed the street to where the house of corrections stood. It was one of the earliest buildings in Titus Bay, much too early for the flimsy wood the tree-cutters now brought for the builders. Like a mountain it stood tall and cold, though conquerable thanks to the key in her hand.

She turned the lock and pulled the door open just enough to let herself in. Just as she wished to not draw the attention of the citizens who lived nearby, she also had to be careful not to alert the other prisoners.

Very little light penetrated the old prison. June only followed what little stone still held the light sneaking in through the door, but that too was lost after a few steps. She continued, her feet landing lighter than leaves in autumn. She had expected it to smell more of unwashed men and was surprised to find the air no less stale than outside. It had only been three days, she supposed.

After a few more paces forward, the moonlight shone through a small window, revealing the iron bars of a cell before her. Lying upon the cold stone was a silhouette, still black in the corner where light could not touch.

"Duncan," she whispered. She watched the sleeping figure rouse, though obviously not aware of her presence. "Duncan, it's me."

"June?"

"Keep your voice down. I'm going to try something." She took hold of the iron mechanism at the edge of the cell door and slid the key in as quietly as she could. The key turned smoothly and the bolt receded, leaving the heavy iron door free to swing.

June pushed the door inward and found his lips in the darkness. At such an intimate distance the smell of three days was all too clear, but she did not mind.

She took his hand. "Let's go. We're leaving Titus Bay."

As they made for the door, he came to a sudden stop. "Where would we go?"

"Anywhere. I don't care if it's the mountains, the foothills, or even the pools in the north. As long as we're together."

"I'm bound for the gallows tomorrow morning. They'll come looking for me and eventually they'll find me. And once they hang me they'll hang you. I can't do that to you, June."

She could not believe what she was hearing. June was risking it all to save him—to save *them*. But that was precisely what he did not want. Duncan worried only for her. He was willing to lose it all to make sure June was safe.

He stood behind the bars and held his hand over hers as he turned the lock back. "My worst fear is coming true. I'm going to be forgotten. I'm going to die before I could make any real impact, too young to even pass my name on to my children. I didn't have time to accomplish anything."

"I'll remember you."

"I know you will." He reached through and stroked her hair. "Ever since I lost my father and mother, I've always felt like I had a hole in the middle of me—some piece of me missing that I desperately needed, but couldn't quite name. You've always done everything you can to fill that hole. You've always been what I needed you to be, June. And so even when I'm long lost to obscurity, I know you'll remember me. I'll always love you for that."

She pleaded with him to come, but he would not. With tears in his eyes he kissed her once more and returned to his dark corner upon the stone.

Back outside, June circled around the building through a narrow alley, her steps deliberate but aimless as she wiped the tears away with the hem of her cloak. She found herself in the square, looking up into the open sky at a moon that seemed more pale than usual. She could hear a sound through the still air, like that of a clock. It could have been no manner of clock June had ever seen before, for in the distance it ticked faster than a heartbeat.

It was not a clock, of course, and once June had

finished wiping the tears from her eyes and had a few moments to calm herself, she recognized the ticks as distant hoofbeats. Across the collapsed market, entering from where the northwest highway met the cobble of the square, she saw a rider. Something about the man rang familiar, and she watched as he directed the beast to meet her.

When the rider was within earshot, he called out, "June, is that you?"

It was the voice of the long-lost bookkeeper proper, Cale the Counter.

"Where have you been? I heard they sent a messenger out to summon you, but no one could find you."

"I'm afraid I haven't been entirely honest about my business in the west, and from what I hear, much has happened while I was away."

"And what were you doing?"

"I went out to find the door in the mountain."

She did not say a word, then. She was too tired. She was tired of sadness, tired of feeling anything. She was tired of the intrigue and disappointment. She was tired of the door in the mountain.

But he could not wait for a response. Leaning down, a man too proud to show his excitement, he then said, "I found it."

24. THE REVELATION OF
CALE THE COUNTER

"What are you saying?"

"Oh, you know the stories, June. Lord Titus's lost door in the mountain. Hector and I have searched for it ever since we were young. The Circle of Scholars published something recently and I did a bit more research on my own. This entire journey was to search for it under the guise of business."

"But," June looked at him sideways, "have you not heard? The circle of scholars...the door...it was a farce." She told him of the rebellion lurking below the surface of Titus Bay, the new mayor and his use of the Circle's false research to distract and discontent the citizens. She admitted that she too thought she had found the door in the mountain herself, even gazed in awe as Mira, by some treacherous wonder, disappeared through it. "But in the end the door proved to hold no wonder at all, for when it burned and fell apart, there was no tunnel behind it. I can't explain where Mira went, but if there was any wonder involved, it must have been in the key—not the door. And it's gone now."

"But, June, the oldest stories spoke of two doors—one in the east and the other in the west. Though I haven't been away on business, I *have* been in the western reaches, and the doors we found were not one in the same."

She gasped at his words, for as soon as they reached her ear she knew them to be true. Mira herself had even said there were two doors, though the old woman had only seen one herself. With the city's entire focus solely in the east, especially after finding the door there, the possibility of a second door had completely slipped from her mind.

"And I agree about the key, by the way. I came to the same conclusion after trying to force the door open for quite some time. It must be bound by some wonder that only Lord Titus's key can unbind."

"The Circle of Scholars had half the city searching their attics and cellars for any old key and turned up nothing. The only key that worked was Mira's, and it disappeared with her behind the first door."

Cale shrugged. "Oh well. Perhaps it will turn up one day. After hearing all that's happened since I've been gone, I can't help but think perhaps I should keep this discovery to myself until things calm down." He touched a binding of rolled parchments hanging from his shoulder. "I had even drawn up maps to submit to the library's records and to the city council."

"So you're content to just let the door be?" She was surprised to hear Cale speak with apathy after obviously having devoted a long journey to the door's discovery. She already knew, from his close friendship to Hector, that he was a regular attendee of the gatherings below the library. And yet he wished his discovery to be known by the city council and accessible to the citizens through the library—completely above board. "You won't even look for the key?"

"It sounds like it isn't the right time for such things. And perhaps this just means the door was not meant for us to go through at all. Perhaps it was just for us to await his return."

His return.

June closed her eyes, trying to remember where she had seen the familiar phrase. Once she could see the inscription, a new plan came to her mind—one that promised more for her and Duncan than simply hiding in the foothills.

"Cale," she said, opening her eyes again, "would you mind if I took one of the maps you've drawn?"

Without a word, he loosened the bindings around the parchments and pulled one from the column. With map in hand, she took a step back. "Let's talk more tomorrow. I'm eager to hear more about your journey." He bid her goodnight and continued along toward the bridge crossing the river to the eastern reaches of the city. Though she knew the next day would find her gone, she could not bear to tell her mentor goodbye. And thus, without a word, she watched him disappear over the crest of the arched bridge.

Retracing her path back to the house of corrections, she again let herself in through the great doors. She strode more boldly in the darkness this time, continuing forth until she saw the light of the moon through the first window.

"Duncan," she whispered. Her hands found the lock her eyes could not, and she let herself into the cell.

She heard a scuffling in the darkness and then Duncan's voice answered. "June? What are you doing back here?"

"I've got a plan. We can be together without fear of being hunted down."

"How?"

"We're leaving Ashmere." She took Duncan's hand and led him out of the black cell and into the night, locking the doors as they left. As they crossed the street to the stone steps leading down past Great Gytha's shop, she told him of her run-in with Cale and showed him the map to the second door in the mountain.

"But it's locked, June. We'll find no passage there, just as we found none the first time."

By this time, they had reached the walkway where Titus's Grave stood. June was distracted from his words, of course, as she wandered about the monument in search of a stone. Crouching down to the edge of the lesser-walked path, she pulled one of the stones from its place and lugged it over.

"I think that when Lord Titus left decades ago," she said, beginning to hoist the stone above her head, "one of his appointed leaders, someone close to him, erected this monument to hold the key he had entrusted to them." She brought the stone down upon the polished epitaph, cracking the surface with a loud thud. Now unconcerned about the noise, she lifted it and let it come down again. The thud was accompanied by a loud ringing sound, and they both looked down to see a key on the ground before them. Disguised as a remarkable sculpture carved into the monument's surface, the real key had been hidden in plain sight for decades.

"I don't believe it," Duncan said, his eyes widening as her slender hand grasped the key they indeed needed to see June's plan through. They hugged and kissed and hopped about with such joy and relief as neither of them had ever felt before. Not only would Duncan's life be spared, but they could be together, unmolested.

Careful not to be overtaken by their love-struck giddiness, June and Duncan hurried up and across the square to fetch horses for their last ride in Ashmere.

25. THE LOVERS' LAST RIDE

Leaving the city, June and Duncan had been nervous that their ride might take them longer than their journey to the first door. Despite Cale's map, which was supremely detailed, neither of them had ever been further west than the city before. Now, hours later, they were surprised to find the western reaches much more plain and hospitable to travelers than the east. The land gently rolled as the highway took them closer and closer to the mountains, until finally leading to the tree-cutters' forest, where the placement of each tree was deliberate, and the organized rows allowed for easy riding.

Even the foothills beyond were friendlier than

their eastern counterparts, and as the map led them from the rigid wood of the tree-cutters into the brush of the mountains, June and Duncan had no problem following the veering paths in the moonlight.

They spent the hours enjoying one another, of course. They spoke of their lives-to-be outside of Ashmere, and wondered what they might find on the other side of the mountain. For how little they remembered of the old world, it was possible the old world might not remember Ashmere at all.

They even mused over the idea that they might not be able to speak to those who lived outside of the hidden country. In the old world, as the stories held, people spoke in different tongues, and they knew not one another's words.

The lovers spoke of those whom they were leaving behind. There had been no time to pack their things, to say goodbye. This was June's single greatest regret already. She would never see her parents again, nor her sister. June was already finding things to be just as Mira said. There truly is no way through life that avoids loss, but also no way that leads to contentment. Every choice is a balance between the two. But just as Mira's door would again open with time, June could still hold out hope that another door might open for her family someday.

The moon was just beginning to disappear over the mountains above them when they finally arrived. Unlike the first, which had necessitated a steep climb to the hidden glade above, the second was easily approached on horseback, the terrain a mixture of grass, tree, and rock that ran straight into a cliff.

That is not to say the location of the door was so immediately evident, or else it might have been found sooner. The door itself was set back within a cleft in the rock, just wide enough for a person to pass through, but not wide enough for a horse. Had Cale not drawn out the scene so well, the lovers themselves might not have found it.

After unsaddling the horses and letting them loose, Duncan took June's hand at the cleft's opening.

"Are you ready?" She looked up into his eyes and knew that he already knew the answer.

"I believe I am."

The last remaining moonlight still shone down through the rocky cleft, and the two lovers made their way deeper until they came at last to the great door that so closely resembled its counterpart in the east. The cold lock turned with Lord Titus's key, and as they pulled the door swung out. June had never been so happy to see darkness in her life. Behind the open door was the tunnel, and as June peered through she almost thought she the distant glimmer of light in the darkness, as if she were looking through to the other side of the mountain.

"I'll go first," Duncan said, "and make sure the path is clear so you don't fall in the dark." He stepped forward, crossing the threshold into the unknown. This was already further than anyone had gone since Lord Titus. Taken completely by the darkness as he proceeded, June heard him call from within, "You know, we should have brought a lantern. This may be a long walk through, but the path is smooth so far."

"I'm coming," she announced, pulling down her hood as she prepared to enter the tunnel. She took the key out of the door and began to pull it shut, so as to lock it from the inside as Mira had done. But as she pulled the iron handle within, the door did not budge.

It was catching on something.

June's heart filled with horror as she looked up to see a gloved hand gripping the edge of the door. Her Uncle Ly emerged from the shadows behind the door, pulling her from the path through the mountain. His handling of her was not in anger. She could see the hurt in his eyes, the pain of betrayal and the dilemma of his appointed office. He was not there to punish her. He was there for Duncan.

At the sudden scuffle, outside, Duncan called back through the tunnel, "June?" At once her worst nightmares came into her mind. She saw Duncan hanging at the gallows. The crowd of citizens cheered as life left his body, before losing interest and returning to their business in the city. Soon it was just her, watching her lover swing with the breeze.

Knowing that Duncan would give himself up once he knew the chief constable had followed them, she leapt to her feet. Lord Titus's key still in hand, she dashed into her uncle's side, sending him stumbling against the jagged stone wall of the cleft. Without a word, she pushed the door shut and leaned hard against it while her shaking hands struggled to find the key's proper place. From behind the door she could hear the muffled shouts of Duncan, and a moment later the chief constable was back upon her, his long arms prying their way between her and the door.

By the time the key finally found its place within the black iron, Duncan had reached the door and was pounding on the inside.

The chief constable clutched her hand upon the key, keeping her from turning it.

"Please, Uncle Ly," she pleaded. Her heart

pounded and her insides burned as she breathed the cold air. "I love him. Please let him go."

"June, I'm sorry. I am. But I have to take him back."

At this she rose to her feet, careful to keep her weight against the door as their hands fought for the iron-ensconced key. Once she had the proper position, she pushed her uncle's hand off the key with her shoulder and turned the key within the lock. The heavy bolt slid and Duncan's pounding immediately stopped. The massive man's hands were back on the key, but before he could do anything June dropped her weight back down, breaking the key off within the lock.

Panting, June leaned back against the now silent door. The chief constable sat with her, likewise winded and catching his breath.

"I'm sorry, Uncle Ly," June said. "I would have done anything to save him, but despite everything I still lost him. You can take me before the council. I'll admit my crime."

The chief constable was silent for some time as he caught his breath. His hands on his knees, his eyes were still as they stared at the ground. He was hard at work thinking, but of what June could not tell. When finally he did again speak, it was in a firm but gentle tone.

"No, June. I'll tell the council Duncan escaped on his own. I'll say I rode out after him but lost his trail in the foothills. They'll want their man, sure enough, but they'll expect him to turn up sooner or later. In such a cramped land as ours, no one stays hidden for long."

26. THE FATE OF
JUNIPER GLADWELL

The next morning, the chief constable informed the council of Duncan's escape. As he had expected, the hangings went on as scheduled, with the chief constable putting out a call for Duncan's capture should any happen upon him. A call that only he and June knew would never be answered.

Life in Titus Bay returned to normal in the months following the rebellion. Recognizing the need for reform, the council soon proposed a change to Ashmere's system of taxes. A simplification, it was to be, and one that would lessen the burden on the guilds and merchants. At the proposal of the guilds, the council even voted to expand to include certain guildmasters, to allow fairness and equity in all decision making. They convened to choose a new mayor from the Norfolk family, remaining true to the design of Lord Titus. They settled on a first cousin, a young man of twenty, and together they vowed to honor Lord Titus's wishes by leading the hidden country in prudence and wisdom.

From then on, the council strove to include the common citizens themselves in all matters of governance. Their first order of business was to decide how to proceed with the city library. With one librarian executed and the other evading capture in the hills, there was no one left to look after it. The doors had remained locked for months. One councilor proposed clearing the books out and using the empty buildings for other purposes, while others insisted the city needed a library to maintain its history and culture.

June raised her hand. She had, by this time, come to terms with a new vision for her life—a life without Duncan. She had, like Great Gytha before her, resolved not to let the tragedy break her. She would carry on.

Standing before the council, June asked humbly that they might make her steward over the library in place of the Westocks. Her request was granted, on one condition: the east wing, the cellar of which had housed the rebellion, would no longer be part of the library. The city would keep it for their own designs.

She happily accepted the terms, the next day handing the crossed quills to Cale the Counter. He was, of course, in utter shock at the news.

"Why, June? You've worked so hard to get here."

"I know, and it was truly worth it. But like you,

I've developed a real penchant for the mysteries of our hidden country. And what better place to search them out? I'll have unlimited time with every book in Ashmere, unknown treasures lost in time."

Ultimately, June got just what she wanted. She spent each day looking after the library, the shelves of which now held all the books of the former east wing. In the evenings, she returned to the cottage next to her parents, a place the children would eventually come Old June's House, having long forgotten Mira's claim on the property. Though Linas with the curious tail made it clear he came and went as he pleased, he was always there when she returned in the evening, glad to curl up next to her as she read in ample candlelight.

Eventually she would come to know each and every text within the library. By that time, of course, her parents had long since passed, and her sister's children had come to live in their late grandparents' cottage. She was an old woman, she knew, but she never lost her resolve. In the eyes of the citizens she had become a scholar in her own right, an authority on all things Ashmere. Even the city council, eventually a group of men much younger than her, would appeal to her knowledgeable counsel. She had lost her Duncan, but she kept his memory alive by accomplishing the work he wanted, and though the citizens knew not her reasons, they adored her for it.

They were not, however, so kind to the memory of her lover. Within her lifetime, the tales warped as they were passed to the next generations, until even *she* could find hardly a semblance of the truth within them. Perhaps it was because the notion of rebellion remained alive in Duncan, for his fate was unknown.

As far as any of them knew, he was still out there. In the passing of but a few decades, history had already forgotten Grant Norfolk. Instead, it had named Duncan the true villain; the man who fled.

June did not know whether to smile or cry; for was not Duncan's greatest desire but to be remembered? In one sense, he got what he wanted. Whereas his father's life had been cut short before he could accomplish anything noteworthy, Duncan, for good or ill, would truly be remembered.

June had a feeling the parents of Ashmere would be whispering the name of Duncan, that specter wandering the foothills, to instill fear in the hearts of their children long after they had forgotten her. She was quite alright with that.

She hoped Duncan would be too.

The End.

ABOUT THE AUTHOR

From his childhood in the Caribbean to a brief stretch in the Eastern Bloc, Tom Lund has found that sometimes the best way to explore this crazy world is to create your own. He attended college in Idaho, where he studied professional and technical writing, but it would not be until nearly five years later that he would venture into the creative realm.

He currently lives in the hills above Saint George, Utah with his wife and son.

Other works by Tom
The Fires of Ashmere

Connect with Tom
www.MrLugg.com

Made in the USA
Middletown, DE
01 June 2019